I dedicate this book to my incredible son, Cree, and my lovely and supportive husband, Cory.
—Tia

To my entire family—my mother, Darlene; father, Timothy; my brothers, Tahj and Tavior; sister, Tia; husband, Adam; son, Aden; and our sweet baby girl.
—Tamera

TIA AND TAMERA MOWRY

TWINTUITION
DOUBLE VISION

HARPER
An Imprint of HarperCollinsPublishers

Library of Congress Control Number: 2014958872
ISBN 978-0-06-237287-1

Typography by Carla Weise
17 18 19 20 OPM 10 9 8 7 6 5 4
❖
First paperback edition, 2016

1

CASSIE

"ARE YOU KIDDING me?" I exclaimed as Mom pulled up beside a small, ramshackle house. "This *so* can't be it."

"Stop it, Cass." My twin sister, Caitlyn, turned and frowned at me from the front seat. "Mom's stopping to check the directions. Right, Mom? I mean, obviously we're not going to live *here*."

Our mother didn't answer as she stared at the house in front of us. If you could call it a house. Neither our bug-specked windshield nor the hazy, late-September Texas air, thick as hot grits, was enough to disguise the ugly little place's crooked shutters, the mold-spotted siding, or the overgrown front yard. Even the driveway was weed choked. It didn't help that every other house on the block was perfect, with fresh paint and a tidy lawn.

Mom's silence confirmed my fears. "Oh, great. Just when I thought things couldn't get any worse."

"Enough, Cassie." Mom's voice was clipped as she cut the engine. Her scarymama voice, Cait and I called it. "It's been a long day, and I'm not in the mood. It might not look quite like it did online, but we'll make it work."

"Yeah," Cait said after a moment. "Um, it has potential. I guess. . . ."

I blew out a sigh of annoyance. Couldn't she admit just once that something wasn't perfect? Cait had always been a glass-half-full kind of girl, but ever since Mom had announced this move—this stupid, crazy-bad-idea move—she'd become even more upbeat than usual.

Me? I'd spent most of the past few weeks locked in my room. Mostly trying to figure out if the state of Texas would allow a not-quite-twelve-year-old to live on her own so that I could stay in San Antonio. Not that Mom would ever allow it. But a girl could dream, right?

Anyway, it was no surprise that my sister and I didn't agree on the move. We didn't agree on much lately. Most people found it hard to believe that we could be so different, especially since we looked so much alike. As identical twins, we had the same big brown eyes, curly dark hair, and skinny legs. We had a few other things in common, too—we both loved dancing, spicy food, and singing in the church choir—but it stopped there.

When it came to our personalities, we were night and day. Our differences hadn't seemed to matter much when we were little; we were best friends and had shared everything. But the older we got, the less time we spent together.

Mom unhooked her seat belt and climbed out

of the car, stretching her arms over her head. It had been a long drive from San Antonio to the middle of freaking nowhere.

I still couldn't believe this was happening. When Mom had retired from the army a couple of years ago, I'd thought it was a good thing. No more worrying about her safety or moving every few years. She could even grow out her hair for a change, give up her boring army buzz and try some kinky twists or extensions, or maybe even a cool Afro.

She *had* grown out her hair a little, but the rest of the plan wasn't progressing quite the way I'd hoped. Mom had decided to go back to school—to the police academy. And when she graduated, it turned out to be harder than she thought to land a job in San Antonio, our home for the past two and a half years—a record for us. Instead she ended up getting recruited to fill a vacant spot in tiny Aura, Texas. Yeah, I'd never heard of it either. Like I said, middle of freaking nowhere.

"So where are the movers?" Caitlyn said, tightening her ponytail elastic. Several curly black tendrils had already escaped and were sticking to her fore-head in the heat. "I thought we were running late."

"We are." Mom sounded grim. "I guess they're late, too."

For a second I kind of pitied the movers. Mom isn't the type of customer who settles for shoddy ser-vice. Almost twenty years in the US Army had made her appreciate promptness. I mean, she was known to ground me and Cait if we were even one second late for curfew.

Not that I would have to worry about that sort of thing anymore. I had a feeling I wasn't going to have much of a social life in this remote town. This did not look like a place fun ever visited.

Forget it, I told myself, kicking a pebble into the long grass. *Play it cool, girl. Mom may have lost her mind, but I'm sure it's temporary. After all, she's a city girl, too. She'll definitely hate it here, which means we'll be back in San Antonio before Christmas.*

The thought made me feel only slightly better. I already missed my friends, my school, my cozy lavender-walled bedroom in our old apartment—my whole life, pretty much. I was sure Cait and Mom had to be feeling the same way, even if they wouldn't admit it.

"Let's take a look inside," Mom said, checking her watch. "The kitchen looked nice in the pictures."

The kitchen was small and dingy, and it looked like there was mouse poop on the stove. Yuck. That just goes to show that you shouldn't believe anything you see online. I hoped there were some decent take-out places nearby.

Mom started opening drawers and peering into cabinets. Dust was flying, making my nose tickle. I stepped past her to look into the living room. Like everything else in the house, it was teeny. The carpet had once been white, or maybe beige, but now it was just plain gross.

"Look, a fireplace!" Cait exclaimed, coming to join me in the archway between the kitchen and living room. "That's cool."

"Yeah, because a roaring fire would really feel awesome right now." I rolled my eyes and wiped the sweat off my forehead. "So where are our rooms?"

"Your bedroom should be at the back of the house." Mom's muffled voice drifted out of the refrigerator.

I followed my sister down the narrow hallway as we explored the place. The first doorway we passed showed a cramped, puke-green-tiled bathroom that looked like it had been installed when my great-grammy Rose was young.

"This is an epic disaster," I muttered.

"Don't be such a downer, Cassie," Cait said. "This isn't the end of the world, you know."

"Whatever," I said, opening the next door we passed. "This one must be Mom's room."

There were two more doors left. When Caitlyn opened the one at the end of the hall, we saw that it led out onto a rickety deck overlooking the backyard.

I opened the remaining door, and inside was a small room containing two twin beds with bare mattresses.

"Wait," Cait said. "Where's the other bedroom?"

"I don't know, but it's got to be better than this one," I said. "I call dibs."

Just then Mom caught up to us. "Listen, girls," she said, clearing her throat. "There's something I've been meaning to tell you. . . ."

Uh-oh. Even Cait looked worried. The last time Mom began a sentence that way was when she first told us we were moving.

"What?" I asked.

"I tried to find a three-bedroom house," Mom said. "But there aren't many rentals to choose from, and we didn't have much time to find something, and, well . . ."

"Hold on," I said. "Are you saying what I *think* you're saying?"

"We have to share a room?" Caitlyn cried out, sounding almost as horrified as I felt.

"Sorry, girls," Mom said, but she didn't sound that sorry. "There's no need to overreact here. You two have shared a bedroom before."

"Yeah, when we were *six*!" I exclaimed. "Get real, Mom. I can't live with her—she's a total slob!"

"Better than being an obsessive neat freak!" Cait shot back, her lower lip quivering.

"Enough." Mom sounded stern. "I don't need a snit right now. You both need to buck up and deal with it."

"No way," I blurted out, tears forming behind my eyes. "Seriously, this has to be a joke."

I could feel my face getting hot, and I knew I had to get out of there fast, before I totally lost it. Pushing past my mother and sister, I raced for the door and ran out.

2
CAITLYN

I WASN'T SURE why Cassie was acting so crazy. Then again, maybe I shouldn't have been surprised. Cass and I used to be like two peas in a pod, but lately I just didn't *get* her. I mean, I wasn't thrilled about sharing a room either. But it wasn't the worst thing ever. It might even be fun, as long as she didn't try to alphabetize my shoes or something.

Mom was rubbing her temples the way she did when one of her headaches was coming on. "I swear, that girl . . . ," she muttered to herself. She caught me looking and straightened up, shoulders squared, military style. "Follow her, Cait," she ordered. "I don't want her getting lost and needing to be brought home by one of the other town cops. Talk about embarrassing."

Going after Cassie was about the last thing I wanted to do. It was hot, I had to pee, and I was totally worn-out from the long car ride. But I wanted to help, for Mom's sake. This move couldn't be easy on her either.

"Sure," I said, forcing a smile as I headed outside. "We'll be back in a sec."

When we were little, Cass and I used to play a game where we took turns guessing what the other was thinking. We called it twintuition. Cute, right? But sometimes it really did feel like we could read each other's minds.

Closing my eyes, I tried to guess which way Cassie had gone, but those days of twintuition were long gone. So I picked a direction at random and headed down the sidewalk. It was Monday afternoon, and the neighborhood was deserted. I felt like the only person in town. The only signs of life were a squirrel dashing across someone's yard and the sound of the cicadas in the trees. I wouldn't have been shocked to see a tumbleweed come rolling down the street.

At the end of the block, I hesitated. If I turned left, I'd be heading back toward the highway. Cassie was upset, but I seriously doubted she would try to walk all the way back to San Antonio. Hitchhike? Also doubtful. Cass liked to act tough, but I knew better.

Glancing in the other direction, I caught a glimpse of store signs in the distance. Jackpot! Cass loved shopping more than life itself.

A few blocks later I reached what had to be the town's main shopping district. Both sides of the street were lined with tall, narrow, old-timey buildings made of brick or stucco and painted in all kinds of fun colors: cream, red, mustard yellow, bright blue. Cute coordinating awnings shaded the glass doors and big picture windows. I spotted a hardware store, a pharmacy, and even a barbershop with an actual striped pole out front. Adorable! There was still no sign of my sister, but I saw several kids around my age hanging out behind a big folding table in front of the Adams General Store.

My heart started beating faster, and for a moment I wanted to turn and run. It was one thing for me to decide that I was going to make the most of this move—that this was a chance for me to reinvent myself, meet new people, have adventures—but it was another thing to *do* it. We'd been in San Antonio for a long time—almost three years. That was almost three years without being the new kids in town, almost three years without having to figure out who was who and what was where and how to make friends fast. I wasn't sure I was ready to start all over again.

Still, I didn't have much choice, right? So I forced myself to smile and walk right up to those kids. I tried to look as friendly as possible.

"Hi there, want to buy some baked goods?" a boy called out. He was skinny, with a big, happy, crooked smile and bright-red hair that looked as if it hadn't seen a comb in a while. "It's for a good cause—we're raising money for the sixth-grade class trip."

Sixth grade. So these were some of my new classmates. Cass and I were supposed to start Aura Middle School on Wednesday.

Meanwhile the two girls next to him kept staring at me. "Who are *you?*" one of them demanded. She had wavy brown hair, a round face, and rosy spots on her cheeks, kind of like a cartoon character. If her expression wasn't cool-verging-on-hostile, I would've called her cute. "I've never seen you before."

"I just moved here." Everyone always says my smile is my best feature, so I made the most of it now, even though she looked about as welcoming as a hill full of fire ants. "I'm Caitlyn Waters."

The other girl looked a little friendlier. Or at least not totally *unfriendly*. She was very pretty and *very* blond. While the other two kids were wearing Aura Middle School T-shirts, she was dressed in an expensive-looking pink beaded tank and a delicate heart-shaped necklace.

"I'm Megan," she said. "That's Lavender and

Liam. So you really just moved here?"

"Yeah. We're waiting for the moving van right now, actually." I pointed to a plate of pastries. "Is that apple strudel? Yum—how much?"

"Two dollars." Lavender sounded kind of aggressive, like she was expecting me to start haggling.

"I'll take one, please." I fished some money out of my pocket and handed it to Liam.

"I made these myself," Megan said as she offered me one of the sticky strudels. "Old family recipe."

"Cool," I said. "I love family recipes. My Maw Maw Jean makes the best hush puppies you ever—"

The rest of the comment caught in my throat. Because right then, as Megan handed me the pastry, something weird happened. Her fingers brushed mine, and my vision suddenly went funky. I found myself looking at two shimmery versions of Megan, one layered on top of the other. One version was dimmed away almost to nothing, as if someone had turned the brightness level on a computer screen all the way down.

The top version was much brighter, almost too

intense to be real. And instead of looking calm and normal, this Megan was red-faced and sweaty, her blond hair disheveled. She seemed as if she was screaming, her mouth open so wide it twisted up her whole face, yet I couldn't hear anything except for a loud buzzing filling my ears.

I gasped as I felt Megan yank her hand out of mine, and the buzzing sound disappeared instantly. Now instead of seeing double, I was face-to-face with all three kids. They stared at me, baffled expressions on their faces.

"Are you okay?" the boy, Liam, asked me.

"Whoa. Why'd she grab your hand, Megan?" Lavender asked.

"I don't know." Megan stepped back, glaring at me with wary blue eyes. "She just went all psycho all of a sudden."

I staggered back a few steps, too. The strudel was lying on the sidewalk. I'd totally lost my appetite.

"S-sorry, it was, uh, the heat," I blurted out as I backed away. I'd never been as good at talking my way out of trouble as Cassie was, and right then my mind went completely blank. "Um, I was, you know..."

I mean, what could I say? I had no idea what had happened.

I only knew it wasn't the first time.

"I—I have to go," I mumbled. I felt my foot slip on the strudel as I spun around, but I caught my balance just in time and took off without a backward glance.

3

CASSIE

WE'D ONLY LIVED in Aura for two full days, but I was already over it. I dragged my feet—as much as I dared in my cute new shoes—as I walked to school with Caitlyn on Wednesday morning. Yes, that's right, I said *walked*. You know all those old people who talk about walking ten miles to school every day, uphill in the snow? Well, switch that to a little over a mile in the soupy, steamy Texas heat. It makes walking feel like swimming in mud. Welcome to my new and not-so-improved life.

"Good thing we won't be here long," I muttered, trying to psych myself up.

"What?" Cait glanced over at me.

"Nothing."

She shrugged and kept walking. We hadn't talked much for the past two days. Not since I'd bolted from the house and discovered there was really nowhere to go. I'd wandered around the pathetic collection of outdated buildings that Aura called a downtown until I ran into Cait. Literally. I'd stepped around a corner just in time for her to practically bowl me over.

Naturally, I'd assumed that Mom had ordered her to track me down, and of course my twin had obeyed, like the good little soldier she is.

Weirdly, though, Cait had barely glanced at me. She hadn't even apologized for plowing into me. Instead she'd muttered something under her breath and hightailed it back to the house. Bizarre. But I'd followed her anyway. What else did I have to do? Besides, if we were going to have to share a bedroom, I wanted to get back in there first and claim the bed by the window.

By the time we'd arrived, the moving van was idling out front and we got busy—sweeping, scrubbing, carrying heavy stuff around, hanging pictures, the works. Mom didn't so much move into a new place as invade it, battering every inch of it into submission. Though actually I didn't mind the work—when I was busy, it was easier to avoid thinking too much about our new life. For now, I tried to focus on the idea that this was temporary. Besides, our new rental needed all the help it could get.

Almost two days later it was time for school. And if my short stint in Aura had convinced me of anything, it was that us living here was *so* not going to work. Mom would have to come to her senses soon and move us back to civilization.

"That must be it," Caitlyn said as we turned the corner past a dusty little diner. "Our new school."

"Thanks, Captain Obvious," I muttered, definitely not in the mood for her chirpy optimism.

Aura Middle School was at the opposite end of town from the hovel Mom called our house. It was a typical school building: boxy and beige and ugly, with columns out front that looked as if someone had stuck them on as an afterthought and lots of narrow windows that looked like eyes glaring down at us.

I shifted my leather messenger bag from one shoulder to the other. The bag had been one of my most awesome finds at my favorite vintage shop back in San Antonio—all my friends had loved it. But if I'd known I'd have to start walking to school, I definitely would've looked for something lighter.

"I guess we should go in and find the office," Caitlyn said. "Mom said they're expecting us."

I nodded, waiting for what came next. What had *always* come next. Our ritual, we called it. See, whenever we started a new school—and that had happened a lot up until Mom had retired from the army—we would take a moment, just the two of us, and hold hands to remind ourselves that we weren't alone in this new place. That we always had each other.

Yeah, I know, pretty lame, right? I'd thought

about telling Cait we could skip it this time—we were getting too old for that sappy stuff. But I didn't have the heart. It meant so much to her.

My fingers twitched as I took a step toward her, waiting for her to grab my hand. But she wasn't even looking at me. "So what are we waiting for?" she said. "Let's go in."

I blinked, so surprised she forgot that I almost blurted out something about our little tradition. But I caught myself. Biting my tongue, I followed her as she headed into the school.

The inside of the building was just as beige and boring as the outside. Well, except for the huge banner hanging over the lobby that read AURA ARMADILLOS in three-foot-high green and gold letters. It featured a giant drawing of a snarling animal with a football tucked under its arm. Beneath the banner, tons of kids were milling around doing their thing. Luckily a big sign on the lobby wall read OFFICE, with an arrow pointing off to the right, which saved us from asking for directions aimlessly, like tourists looking for the Alamo.

The lady behind the desk had pink hair. Not in a cool punk-rock kind of way, just very . . . *pink*. It looked like cotton candy that somebody had lacquered into the shape of a pumpkin. Or maybe it was supposed to be a crouching armadillo? Who knew? She barely glanced up from her computer as we told her who we were and where we'd come from. Cait is way better at talking to adults, so I hung back and let her take the lead.

"Welcome to AMS, hons," the woman drawled. "Here are your schedules. Let us know if we can help out, mm-kay?"

"Thanks," Cait said, even though Pink Lady had already returned her full attention to her screen. Picking up one of the sheets, Cait consulted it carefully. "It says my locker is in East Hall One," she said. "Where's yours?"

I grabbed the other sheet and scanned it as we wandered out of the office. Kids were streaming past us in every direction, some slowing down to give us curious looks. Ignoring them, I focused only on my sister.

"West Hall Two," I said. "Not that I have any clue where that is."

"Let's ask somebody," Cait said. But as she turned around, a guy suddenly called out her name.

It was weird, considering we didn't know another soul in Aura. Turning, I saw a skinny redhead coming toward us. He wore weird plaid shorts and a huge, dorky grin. If there was a picture beside the word *nerd* in the dictionary, this kid would be it.

He saw me, too, and stopped short. "Whoa," he exclaimed, looking from me to Cait and back again. "You're twins!"

"What gave it away?" I said, rolling my eyes.

Cait smiled uncertainly. "Hi," she said. "It's Liam, right? And, yeah, this is my sister, Cassie."

"Nice to meet you, Cassie. Liam O'Day, at your service." He actually stuck out his hand to shake. Who *does* that? I stared at his hand until he put it away.

He shrugged, then turned to Cait. "So, are you guys in sixth grade? What homeroom?"

Caitlyn checked her sheet again. "Um, it says Ms. Xavier?"

"Cool! That's my homeroom, too." He seemed way too excited about it. "I'll show you guys how to get there."

"Not me," I said as I glanced at my own sheet again. "I've got Mr. Bustamonte."

"Can you maybe tell us where our lockers are first?" Cait asked Liam, showing him our sheets. "I want to make sure I can work my combination."

"Those lockers are at opposite ends of the school, pretty much," Liam said. "Which should I show you first?"

"You don't need to show me mine," I said quickly. "Point me in the right direction and I'm good to go." Being the new kid so often had taught me that first impressions were everything. If the rest of the school saw me walking around with this Liam kid, I was definitely going to be labeled a geek before the first bell.

Unfortunately, that kind of stuff never seemed to occur to Cait until it was too late. She was already peering down the hallway past the office. "That sign says *east*," she said. "Is that where I go?"

"Uh-huh." Then Liam waved a skinny, freckled hand toward a stairwell on the opposite side of the lobby. "Your locker is that way. Second floor," he told me, then turned and led Cait away.

"Gee, don't worry about me, sis, I'll be fine," I muttered. Whatever. Like I said, I wasn't interested in joining the Nerd Patrol, even if I wouldn't be here that long. I was pretty sure I could manage to locate my locker without an escort. But it wouldn't have hurt Cait to say good-bye.

As I headed up the stairs, I tried to check out the locals without making it obvious. There seemed to be the usual mix: jocks, hicks, nerds, normal kids. Most of them ignored me aside from a few curious glances. But one kid actually stepped over and blocked my path as I started to pass him on the stairs. The guy really stood out from the rest of the kids in his clunky cowboy boots, messily slicked-back hair, and a leather jacket that looked way too hot for the weather.

"Hey, you! You new here?" the kid demanded, sounding kind of aggressive.

I met his gaze evenly, not wanting him to think I was intimidated by the Billy-the-Kid-meets-*Grease* thing he had going on.

"Who wants to know?" I demanded in return.

"Look out, Gabe!" a girl exclaimed, barreling down the steps clutching a cello case. "Coming through!"

The kid jumped aside, cursing at the girl as her cello almost clocked him. I took the opportunity to keep moving, not looking back. Great. If everyone here was as friendly as Greasy Gabe, I was in for an even more fabulous time at this school than I'd feared.

As I emerged from the stairwell onto the second floor, I noticed a girl leaning over the water fountain. Wavy brown hair cut into a cute shoulder-length style. Surprisingly stylish clothes for this dusty small town. I even liked her shoes. Okay, this was more like it. Maybe the natives here weren't totally hopeless after all, because anyone who dressed like that definitely had potential.

I walked over and cleared my throat. "Hey," I said. "I'm new here. Can you—"

She didn't even let me finish. As soon as she turned and saw me, her hazel eyes widened dramatically.

"Oh, no way," she said loudly. "I can't *even* believe you're talking to me. Sorry, I don't talk to freaks!"

Spinning on her heel, she took off down the hall. I was too stunned to respond. Why had she called me a freak? For a moment I wasn't sure whether to yell back at her or burst into tears.

But no. A few kids were already staring, and I wasn't about to cry in front of them. Besides, why should I? I'd never even seen that girl before! Where did she get off calling me names?

I hadn't been in the best mood to start with, and now I was steaming. It really was going to take all I had to survive this stupid place.

I spun in the opposite direction, fuming, just as someone stepped toward the water fountain. I crashed into him—hard.

"Oof!" I blurted out, ready to tell off the person who had gotten in my way.

But the words died in my throat the minute I got a load of my victim. He was tall and lean and absolutely adorable, with wavy dark hair and a green-and-gold letterman jacket.

"Sorry," he said, with a dimply smile that made him look even cuter. "You okay?"

I guess I looked a little wobbly, because he reached out and touched my arm to steady me. The minute I felt his touch, all the breath in my body whooshed out of me and my vision sort of flickered like a busted laptop screen and for a second I was seeing double. Oh, no. Seriously, please, no! This couldn't be happening, not right now. . . .

But it was. I suddenly found myself looking at two versions of Cute Jock's hand. One of them was fading so far into the background I could hardly see it, and the other was much brighter, freaky-bright—and tightly clutching my own hand, as if he didn't want to let me go.

A distant voice floated through my head, though

it was hard to hear over the buzzing sound filling my ears. "Are you okay?"

With great effort I ripped my arm away, and just like that the image of his hand holding mine disappeared. Cute Jock gazed down at me, his face a mixture of confusion and concern.

"S-sorry, dude," I managed to say, in something almost resembling a normal voice. "I spaced out there for a sec."

"Oh. I haven't seen you around before. I'm Brayden."

I opened my mouth, trying to dredge up my own name. The vision had left my brain a tangled mess. But before I could speak, I heard a shrill voice nearby.

"Ew, Brayden, stay away from the new girl!"

It was Wavy-Hair Girl. She was barreling toward me with a pretty blonde hot on her heels.

"Hi, Lavender," Brayden said. "So did you already meet, uh . . ." He turned to me. "What was your name again?"

"Her name is Psycho Freak," Lavender spat out.

"What's your problem?" I demanded. "Do I know you?"

"Are you serious? I already knew you were a complete weirdo, but—" Lavender began.

The other girl plucked at her friend's sleeve. "Come on, Lav," she interrupted. "We don't have time for this. I still need to cram for that English test."

"English test?" Brayden looked alarmed. "Oh, man, I forgot that was today. I've gotta go study—if my grades slip, my folks will be steamed. They might even make me quit the team!"

"Oh, please." Lavender rolled her eyes and smiled at him as the three of them walked off together, not sparing a backward glance for me. "You're, like, the smartest guy on the entire football team. I'm sure your parents will get over it if you get an A minus this time."

So Brayden was on the football team—and he was smart, too? Very interesting.

But no. I wasn't going to let myself get distracted

by a guy, no matter how cute. No matter how much that image of holding hands with him made me shiver. I would need all my energy to survive this stupid town, for however long I was stuck here.

And while I was at it, maybe I could figure out why my brain had decided to start randomly shorting out lately—and why it seemed to be getting worse. Because I was starting to feel secretly worried that I really *was* becoming some kind of psycho freak.

4
CAITLYN

"HERE WE ARE," Liam announced, leading me into the classroom. "Your new homeroom."

I smiled at him. "Thanks for showing me the way."

"Sure. Want to sit with us? Me and Bianca, I mean. We always sit here in the front."

He headed toward a dark-haired girl bent over a book. I followed, feeling almost normal. It was amazing how one friendly face could help change your attitude.

Especially since Liam hadn't even mentioned the embarrassing incident the other day. Ever since having that weird vision, I'd been pretty nervous about starting school. Why did something like that have to happen in front of three soon-to-be classmates? It was bad enough it was happening at all.

I squeezed my eyes shut for a second, trying not to think about it. But it was getting harder and harder each time to blame it on being tired, hungry, or wired from too much sugar.

The first time it had happened, maybe six months earlier, I'd actually thought it was a dream. I'd had the flu, and awakened from a restless sleep to find my mom pressing her hand against my forehead, checking my fever. The weird buzzing noise had kicked in with a frenzy, and my vision swam. There seemed to be two Moms leaning over me—one of them looked concerned, while the other was smiling. The two versions fought for my attention until she finally left the room and I drifted back to sleep.

I'd forgotten all about it until it happened a second time—only this time I'd been wide awake. I was at the dentist's office, and the hygienist had just stuck her hands in my mouth, ready to go to work. All of a sudden two versions of her came into view. One version of the hygienist was fainter as she peered at my teeth and chatted while the other version of her was laughing hysterically. It lasted until she stepped back to let me rinse, and I felt paralyzed, shocked by the whole experience.

Finally, there was the weirdest one—the thing with Cass. It was a couple of days before Mom told us about the move. Cassie had been studying for the first big social studies test of the year and was kind of freaking out about it—social studies wasn't her best subject. So I'd given her my notes to help her out, but when her hand brushed against mine, suddenly there were two versions of my twin facing me. One still looked grumpy and worried, and sort of faded into the background, while the other, a much happier Cass, was waving a test paper in front of me with a big, blue A scrawled at the top. That Cass was so bright she didn't look real.

I guess Cass noticed I was acting strange,

because she abruptly yanked her hand away and told me I was freaking her out, staring like that. So I joked that I was practicing positive thinking, trying to imagine her doing a great job on the test. But you know what? It actually happened. Two days later we got those tests back, and Cass got an A, just like in my vision. Weird coincidence, right?

And weird enough to make me feel more than a little uneasy. Especially since the vision of Cass had been the brightest and strongest yet.

As those memories skittered through my mind, we reached Liam's desk. There weren't many other students in the room yet, but his friend Bianca looked as if she'd settled in awhile ago. A book was open in front of her, and she was sipping from a water bottle as she read. She was short and slim, with sleek dark hair pulled back from her face and a mishmash of colorful plastic barrettes. Her feet were resting on an instrument case under the desk.

"Hey, Bianca," Liam said loudly as he collapsed into his seat. "There's a new student. Caitlyn Waters, meet Bianca Ramos."

Bianca stuck a finger between the pages of her book, clearly marking her place. She studied me, looking me up and down. She didn't smile, but didn't frown either.

"Hi," she said in a quiet, surprisingly deep voice. "Welcome to Aura. Where'd you come from?"

"San Antonio," I replied. "We moved here two days ago."

"Here—sit between us so we can both talk to you." Liam lunged out of his seat, moving over.

"Thanks." I sat down in the vacant chair and set my backpack on the desk. More kids were streaming in.

"San Antonio, huh?" Liam said. "That's cool. That's where we're going for our class trip—you know, the one we were raising money for the other day?"

My smile wavered slightly. That was his first mention of the Incident. But still, he looked friendly and normal, and not at all judgy. Maybe it hadn't been as bad as I'd thought. Maybe if Liam had already forgotten about it, those girls would, too.

Maybe someday soon we'd all be laughing about it together.

"Yeah, I remember you guys mentioning the class trip," I said cautiously. "Um, so those girls you were with—are you guys all pretty good friends?"

Bianca's gaze had drifted back to her book, but now she glanced at Liam with interest. "Which girls?" she asked him. "I thought you were working the grocery store with Josh and Goober."

"Nuh-uh." Liam shrugged. "Ms. Xavier said they had enough people, so she asked me to team up with Megan March and Lavender Adams."

Bianca let out a snort. "Oh. Poor you."

Okay, so they *weren't* all friends. I probably shouldn't have been surprised. Mom always told us not to judge people by their appearances, but Cassie claimed she could spot a nerd at fifty paces. And as much as I liked him, I had to admit that Liam was, well, not particularly un-nerdy, if you know what I mean. And now that I thought about it, Megan and Lavender hadn't really seemed like the kind of girls who hung out with people like him.

I looked up as three boys rushed in, talking and laughing loudly. They were all probably twice Liam's size, but besides their broad shoulders and long legs, they didn't look much alike. One boy was super pale, with light-blond hair and blue eyes. The second had olive skin and wavy brown hair, and the third had even darker skin and super-close-buzzed hair.

They jostled and shoved one another playfully as they made their way to the back of the room. Another boy had stalked in just ahead of them. "Watch it, Jock Breath," he said with a scowl as the blond kid bumped into him. The kid who'd spoken was short and beefy, with greasy brown hair and jeans tucked into his cowboy boots.

The jocks ignored him completely, and the kid's scowl grew even darker. He stomped to a desk near the windows and slammed his books onto it.

"That's Gabe," Bianca said quietly. "He's got an attitude about the B Boys." She grimaced. "And everything else, too, pretty much."

"The B Boys?" My gaze shifted back to the three jocks who were taking their seats in the back row.

"That's what everybody calls them," Liam said. "Their names are Buzz, Biff, and Brent." He ticked off each name on one skinny finger. "Plus Brayden, of course, but he's not in this homeroom. But they're all on the football team together."

"Yeah," Bianca said. "Gabe tried out for the team, but he got cut."

Liam nodded. "Everyone was pretty surprised since his uncle was the star of the team back in his day."

"Right," Bianca said. "And nobody was more surprised than Gabe." The corners of her mouth twitched, though it didn't quite turn into a smile. "Ever since, Gabe's really had it in for the guys who made it—not that they seem to notice or care."

"So football is a big deal here, huh?" I said, my mind drifting to the games and pep rallies at my old school, which had always been super fun.

This time Bianca's mouth twitched all the way into a wry half smile. "What do you think? This is Texas." She turned to Liam. "So how were Megan and Lav? I'm surprised you survived a whole afternoon with them."

"Are those two really that bad?" I asked, trying to sound casual.

"Megan's okay, mostly," Liam said. "She's probably the most popular girl in the sixth grade. Her family practically founded this town back in the Alamo days." He hesitated. "And Lavender is, um—"

"Here," Bianca interrupted, nodding toward the door.

Looking over, I saw Lavender walking in with a couple of other girls. She saw me, too.

"How'd you get here so fast, freak?" she said loudly, glaring at me.

For a second I didn't understand what she meant. It had been like a day and a half since I'd seen her at the fund-raising stand.

"Didn't you hear me?" she said when I didn't answer, her voice getting even louder. "I said, how'd you get here before me? I came straight from the stairs, and you were standing there like a doofus when I left."

Wait. Oh. Right.

"Uh, that was probably my sister," I said.

"Yeah," Liam piped up. "They're identical twins! We've never had twins in our class before."

"Twins?" one of the other girls said in surprise.

"Twins," Lavender said, like it was some kind of disease. "So which one of you was the freak I met on Monday?"

"That would be me," I admitted weakly. "Sorry about that. I guess the heat got to me, and—"

Catching movement out of the corner of my eye, I turned and saw that Mr. Bad Attitude, Gabe, had shot up in his chair. "Wait, did somebody say twins?" he called out. "Where?"

"Here," I said, glad for an excuse to turn away from Lavender. "My sister, Cassie, and I just moved to town, and—"

"I know who you are!" Gabe leaped to his feet, stomping toward me, his boots clomping on the tile floor. "Your mom stole my uncle Chuck's job!"

"What?" I blurted out, having no idea what he was talking about. Judging by the expressions on Liam's and Bianca's faces, they didn't know either.

But it definitely couldn't be good news.

"Chill out, Gabe." Lavender rolled her eyes. "I'm trying to deal with this freak, okay?"

"Get in line," Gabe snarled. "Because if I have anything to say about it—"

"Attention, people!" a woman cried, striding into the room with her long, peasant-style dress flowing around her. "Take your seats; we have business before the announcements come on."

Most of the kids scattered, even Lavender, though she shot me one last dirty look as she went. Only Gabe was left standing, beefy fists clenched at his sides.

"Mr. Campbell?" the teacher said, arching a drawn-on eyebrow at him. "Seat. Now."

"Yes, Ms. Xavier," Gabe muttered. But even as he stalked back to his seat, I could feel him glaring at the back of my head.

I tried to focus on the teacher as she beamed at me, clasping her hands in front of her. Every one of her fingers had a ring on it, most of them chunky and boho looking, with huge, colorful stones. Ms. Xavier looked like she should be selling pottery or beaded jewelry in La Villita or Southtown, not teaching sixth grade in a small town. Her reddish-brown hair sprang out from her face in wild curls, and her Birkenstocks revealed that every toenail was painted a different color. She was awesome!

"You must be Caitlyn Waters," she said. "Welcome to Aura Middle School!"

"Thanks," I said. By now almost all the seats were full, and I could feel every set of eyes trained on me. I had an idea I knew what was coming next. . . .

"Why don't you stand up and tell us all a little bit about yourself, Caitlyn?" Ms. Xavier said cheerfully.

Yup. Why did teachers always do that to the new kid? And this time I didn't even have Cassie standing beside me. I wondered if another teacher was humiliating her in some other classroom right this second. Knowing I might as well get it over with, I crawled to my feet and forced a smile.

"Hi, y'all," I said as cheerfully as I could. "Like she said, I'm Caitlyn Waters."

I was trying not to meet anyone's eye, but I

couldn't help seeing that Lavender was still making smirky little faces at me. Turning to Liam and Bianca, I focused on them instead. Liam looked as friendly as ever, and Bianca gave me a nod and a small, sympathetic smile.

"So about me . . ." Even though Mom liked to claim I never stopped talking, I was never sure what to say in moments like this. Somehow I doubted anyone cared that I loved funny movies and dried chili flakes on my popcorn, or that I was a teensy bit afraid of squirrels. "I moved here from San Antonio, and I have an identical twin sister named Cassie," I said. "I like to sing, and I played softball and ran track at my old school. Um, and—"

"Identical twins?" Ms. Xavier broke in. "How fascinating! Did you know that in the voodoo religion, twins are revered and thought to have supernatural powers?"

Cass and I had heard a lot of wacky stuff about twins over the years, but that was a new one. Luckily I was saved from having to respond when the PA system crackled to life.

"Time to take your seat, Ms. Waters," the teacher said. "And again, welcome."

I sank gratefully back into my chair. The announcements began—I recognized the cheery, slightly nasal voice of the pink-haired lady who had given us our schedules. She started with that day's cafeteria menu, then mentioned a pep rally and home football game on Friday, which brought loud whoops from the back of the room.

Once again I thought back to my old school. Football games were one of the few things Cassie and I had still done together. We'd meet up with a whole gang of friends at someone's house, drink soda until we were totally jazzed on caffeine and sugar, and then scream our hearts out for the home team. It was a total blast!

Would football games be anything like that here? Would Cass even want to go? She seemed to have a pretty bad attitude about Aura so far. Would games still be as much fun without her? Thinking about it made me feel lonely and sort of squirmy, so I did my best to push it out of my mind.

Of course, not thinking about the past left me with only the present—including what had just happened. I knew why Lavender thought I was a freak, but what had Gabe's comment been all about? The only thing Mom had told us about her new job was that someone had left the squad, creating an opening. So how could she have stolen the job from Gabe's uncle or anyone else?

I had no idea, and it was just one more reminder that life was different now. Whether I liked it or not.

5

CASSIE

BY FRIDAY AFTERNOON I'd figured out where most
of my classes were—not much of a challenge since
Aura Middle School was tiny compared to our last
school. As in seriously tiny. At AMS the entire sixth
grade was divided into only two sections—green
and gold—with only one homeroom per section.
That was it. The sections stayed separate for most
of their classes, coming together only for lunch and
gym, and mixing it up for electives.

The good news? Lavender wasn't in my section.

The bad news? Her blond friend—who I quickly learned was named Megan March—was, along with a couple of girls who I could only assume were her minions. Their favorite activity, especially during homeroom and study hall, seemed to be whispering to one another while staring at me. Nice, right? It hadn't taken me long to figure out that Lavender's bad attitude had something to do with my sister. I had no idea what Caitlyn had done to get her all worked up—or when, for that matter. But whatever it was, Lavender and Co. were definitely holding it against me.

For one thing, I was pretty sure they were behind the ridiculous rumors flying around school, like the ones where Cait and I were only here in Aura because we got kicked out of our old school for cheating or shoplifting or beating up a teacher. Or the one about how we weren't just regular twins but conjoined twins who'd had surgery to separate us since we'd been born joined at the butt. Pretty juvenile stuff, right? Even so, apart from Cait's nerd troop, the kids at school were giving us a wide berth.

It was more than a little distracting. But at least I was ahead on most of the class material and caught up quickly on the rest. Even social studies wasn't so bad. I spent half of Friday's class doodling the San Antonio skyline in the margins of my notebook. It turned out pretty well, if I say so myself. I gazed at it, imagining myself back there, having a real life instead of being stuck here in Atrocious Aura.

The bell jolted me out of my fantasies. Everyone immediately started shuffling around, jamming papers and books into their bags, getting ready to bolt.

"All right, people," the social studies teacher said. Her name was Ms. Xavier, and she was as weird as the rest of the town was boring. Totally wackadoodle, actually, from her long, crazy rat's nest of dark hair to her so-last-season flowy gypsy skirts. Trying to calculate how many fashion faux pas she made per day made it a little easier to stay awake in her class. "Finish the reading this weekend, all right?" she said, winking at us. "But don't worry; you can start it after the game this afternoon. I'll see y'all there, right?"

I winced as the boy behind me whooped directly into my ear. All around the room, people cheered or shouted, "Go, Armadillos!" I'd thought kids at my old school were into football. But here? It was practically a religion. Turning, I saw that Brayden was trading high fives with his friends at the back of the room.

Yeah, he was in my section, too. It had taken me about zero point five seconds to notice that when I'd walked into my first class. Not that it mattered. I wouldn't be here long enough to care.

I stuffed my books into my bag as the other kids rushed for the door. Out of the corner of my eye, I saw someone coming my way and braced myself.

But it wasn't Megan, or even my teacher. It was Brayden. He bent down with one quick move, surprisingly graceful for such a tall guy, and grabbed something off the floor by my feet.

It was a pen. "Hey," he said, holding it out. "I think you dropped this."

"Thanks." I carefully took the pen, trying not to let my hand touch his. The last thing I needed right now was for that weirdo double vision thing to happen again. Wednesday's disaster with Brayden was the third or fourth time something crazy like this had happened over the past six months or so, and it was starting to freak me out.

At first I'd thought it was just low blood sugar. It was a Saturday back in the spring, and I'd gone to the mall with a few friends. We'd spent the day on a major shopping spree, and I was shaking with hunger by the time we finally hit the food court.

I'd been standing in line, counting the seconds until I could sink my teeth into my favorite Cajun chicken wrap. But I guess I'd reached for my food a little too eagerly, because I accidentally grabbed the guy's hand behind the counter instead.

And that's when it happened. The moment I touched his hand, my brain sort of shorted out, and my vision went fuzzy. Suddenly his bored expression transformed briefly into a terrified one. I pulled back in shock, but the whole thing only lasted a split second. I'd figured it was just hunger making me hallucinate.

Until it happened again. This time with Mom. I was helping her peel potatoes for dinner. Our kitchen in the old apartment was pretty small, so we were right next to each other. Our shoulders bumped, and suddenly I heard the buzzing sound again. When I glanced over at Mom, there were *two* of her. One version, faded away almost to nothing, looking normal, while the other looked really worried, freaked-out even—which isn't like Mom, who always stays cool as a cucumber even when everything's melting down around her. I hated seeing her like that and shrank back quickly. Once our shoulders parted, the vision was gone. Mom hadn't even noticed anything had happened!

I had to admit, it was getting even harder to ignore that something very weird was going on. Especially since it occurred a couple more times— and each time it lasted a little longer, and the strange vision got a little more vivid.

And now it had happened again, right here in Aura. With Brayden. And that vision of us holding hands. It seemed so real. I mean, I didn't totally hate the idea of holding hands with Brayden, but still it was eerie. It definitely didn't seem like a random daydream. I mean, sure, Brayden was cute. But I wasn't the type of girl who went around imagining herself holding hands with every cute guy I saw. So what was going on with me? And how could I keep it from happening again?

Even though I tried to avoid it, Brayden's fingers did sort of brush lightly against my hand. I braced myself for the buzzing sound, but luckily nothing strange happened. Except that Brayden kept standing there, sort of rocking back and forth on his heels and smiling down at me. What was that about?

"Well, okay," he said after a long, awkward moment. "See you in art, I guess."

"Yeah," I said.

He started to turn away, then paused. "And listen, you should come to the game today," he said. "Like Ms. X said, everyone goes. It's pretty fun." He puffed out his chest. "And we're totally going to crush West River; half their good players graduated last year, and—"

"Yo, Diaz!" one of the other jocks shouted. "You coming?"

"Yeah." Brayden shot me one last smile, then loped off. "I'm coming."

I held my breath, watching him go. He really was awfully cute. For a moment I was tempted. What would be the harm in going to the football game? It might even be a fun distraction. A decent way to pass the time until I got myself out of this speed bump of a town.

Then I saw Megan March and one of her minions lurking in the doorway. Were they watching me, or was I paranoid? I caught Megan's eye, and she whipped around, blond hair flying, to whisper something in her friend's ear. The other girl giggled. I was *so* not being paranoid.

Part of me wanted to find a place to hide. But the bigger part, the part that always wanted to be the best, wasn't having any of it. No small-town twit was going to intimidate *me*! I mean, come on!

I grabbed the rest of my stuff and strode toward the door. Megan and Minion were still hanging out in the doorway. I brushed past them with an icy cool "Excuse me."

"There's no excuse for you," the minion piped up.

It was such a lame, elementary-school response that I almost laughed. Almost. Instead I kept on going without a backward glance.

As I rounded the corner, I had to stop short to keep from running right into my twin and her new Super Nerd Squad. She'd been hanging around nonstop with Liam, and I guess he and this Bianca girl were a package deal. I didn't know much about her except that she had a clarinet case permanently glued to one hand and a book affixed to the other. I wasn't a hundred percent sure she could talk, since I hadn't heard a peep out of her yet.

"Cass!" Cait said, actually sounding happy to see me.

I couldn't imagine why. We'd barely spoken all week. Which was a little awkward, given our current sleeping arrangements. She'd actually tried to start some chitchat after lights-out a few times, but I'd fake-snored until she gave it up. I wasn't in the mood for any late-night sisterly bonding, especially when she was acting too happy about moving to Aura to commiserate with me about how awful it was.

"Funny, I was just thinking about you," I snapped, glaring at her.

"Really?" She looked surprised. "What do you mean?"

I can really turn on the sarcasm when I want to. And right then I let it flow. "I mean, I was thinking how grateful I am that I have the exact same face as you," I said. "That way whenever anyone sees me, they think about whatever wackadoodle thing you did the other day. Thanks a lot. Now they're starting to think I'm just as big a weirdo as you."

"What's she talking about?" Liam asked. "Oh, wait, is this about the—"

Cait shushed him abruptly. She frowned at me, arms akimbo. "And I'm sure none of this has anything to do with your bad attitude about this town."

What do you know? My sweet sister could pull out the sarcasm, too! If I'd been in a better mood, I might have been impressed. "Whatever,"

I said. "I just wish you—"

Before I could finish, someone came barreling down the hall. Uh-oh—it was Gabe, the greasy-headed cowboy.

"Out of my way, losers," he snarled, pausing to glare at me and Caitlyn as he shoved past us.

"What's with that guy anyway?" I muttered.

"That's Gabe," Liam said in his ooh-ooh-I-know-the-answer way.

"Yeah," Bianca spoke up. "He thinks your mom stole his uncle's job or something."

"What?" I was so surprised to hear her say anything that it took a second for her words to sink in. I glanced at Cait, who looked uneasy.

"I don't know what that's about either," she said quickly. "It's probably nothing."

"Yeah, keep telling yourself that, Sunshine," I said with a snort.

But I didn't really care what Gabe's problem was. I just wanted out. As in out of stupid Aura, Texas. For good.

And the sooner, the better.

6
CAITLYN

"SO ARE YOU guys going to the game this afternoon?" I asked Liam and Bianca as the final bell rang.

Liam wrinkled his nose. "Football? No thanks."

I shouldn't have been surprised. Liam wasn't shy about sharing his interests in all kinds of things, from science fiction movies to current events, but he hadn't mentioned sports at all. Still, I couldn't help being a little disappointed. What fun was a football game without good friends to share it with?

I turned to Bianca. "What about you? Want to

go with me? It'll be fun, right?"

"I'll be there." She held up her clarinet case. "I'm in the band. Sorry, but we're not allowed to have anyone sit with us."

She actually did sound sorry. Bianca didn't have a whole lot to say, since she let Liam do the talking for her most of the time, but I liked her. She was smart, and thoughtful, and maybe a little quirky—my kind of people.

"Bummer," I said, trying to hide my disappointment. "Oh, well, Mom will probably want me to help finish some home improvement projects this afternoon anyway."

"What about your sister?" Liam said as he gathered up his papers, which looked as if they'd exploded all over his desk. "Can't you go with her?"

"Sure, maybe." I forced a smile. Cass and I had hardly spoken all week. For some reason she seemed to blame me as much as Mom for this move, probably because I wasn't being all bratty about it like she was. I was sure she thought I was faking it whenever

I acted like this move wasn't the worst thing ever. So what if I was a little, at first? What was so wrong with looking on the bright side?

Still, I was starting to think it was time for me and Cass to kiss and make up. I looked for her outside of school, but there was no sign of her. By the time I got home she was flopped on her bed, flipping through a fashion magazine.

"Hi," I said, trying to sound upbeat. "So, listen, I was thinking."

"You probably shouldn't do that." She turned the page so fast I heard it tear. "Every time I think about my life, I want to cry."

"Yeah." I took a deep breath. "About that. We should probably try to make the best of things, you know? For real. And what better way to do that than by going to the football game today? I hear almost everybody in town is going."

She rolled over and gazed at me. "That just goes to show that there's nothing to do in this stupid place."

"Come on, Cass." I sat down on the edge of my bed. "You like football, remember? We always had a blast at the games."

"That was before." She turned away, burying herself in her magazine. "When I liked our school. And actually had friends."

Her tone was chilly. But I knew my sister, and I was pretty sure she wanted to make up as much as I did.

"Come on, Cass," I wheedled. "We should at least go check it out. We don't have to stay if it's lame."

She glanced at me with a little frown. "Sorry. Not in the mood."

"Don't be like that!" I said as my voice became shrill. "For real, Cass—let's go to the game and try to have fun, okay? What's the worst that could happen?"

Mom stuck her head in the doorway, her face serious. "What are you girls talking about?" she asked in a tone that said she already knew. "Do you need a ride to the football game?"

"No," Cassie said. "At least I don't. I'm not going."

"Why not?" Mom stepped into the room. She looked crisp, professional, and a little intimidating in her new police uniform with the shiny gold star on her chest. "I hear the games are the place to be on the weekends around here. It would be good for you girls to go. Help you settle in and feel a part of things."

"I know," I said. "I'm trying to talk Cass into it."

"And she's failing," Cass said. "I'm not interested. Seriously."

Mom eyed her. "Well, maybe you should *get* interested," she said. "Seriously."

Cassie sat up, looking stubborn. "What are you going to do, *order* me to go to the game, Officer Waters?" she said, her voice dripping with attitude.

Uh-oh. Mom hated when we sassed her like that. I braced myself for yelling, but instead Mom's voice got very quiet—which was even scarier.

"What's in order here, young lady, is a better outlook," she told Cass. "It would do you good to get out of the house and see more of your new hometown." She checked her watch. "Get your shoes on, and I'll drop you both off on my way to work."

"But——" Cassie began.

Mom raised an eyebrow. "Shoes. Car. Now."

Ten minutes later Mom was pulling into the high school parking lot. The middle school team practiced on the dusty field right behind the school, but games took place at the high school's stadium a few blocks away. The place was crammed with cars and pickup trucks, all of them decorated with green and gold ribbons or big Armadillo stickers on the windows. People were streaming toward the bleachers, and the crowd was huge. Aura had a pretty serious stadium for such a small town—it was almost as big as the one at our old school, though the bleachers were a little shorter and didn't go all the way around. Still, it was obvious everyone took football seriously.

"Let's go," I said with a shiver of nerves.

"Whatever." Cass took her time unhooking her seat belt and hauling herself out of the car. Still, I caught a flicker of interest in her eyes as she glanced toward the bleachers. Maybe she didn't hate being here as much as she was letting on.

Nobody paid us much attention as we headed in. I only recognized a few faces from school. There were lots of adults in the stands, and plenty of high schoolers, too.

The game had already started, though according to the armadillo-shaped scoreboard we'd only missed a few minutes. "Wow, this place is packed," I said as the crowd let out a cheer for a first down. "I hope we can find seats."

Cassie looked dubious as she scanned the home-side stands. "I don't know," she said. "If it's too crowded, we could probably walk back to that fast-food place we passed."

"No way!" I grabbed her hand, pulling her farther in. "We'll find space."

It looked like everyone in town was crammed onto the bleachers! The only empty seats were on the opposite side, where the visiting team's fans sat. Not that I was going to sit with our rivals. That definitely *wasn't* the way to fit in.

We wandered back and forth in front of the stands for a moment, hoping someone would take pity on us and make room. Cassie was actually watching the game, her eyes on the quarterback getting ready to snap the ball. Now, if I could find us somewhere to sit fast, before she lost interest . . .

I paused in front of some slightly older kids who were sort of sprawled across a bench a few rows up.

"Hey, y'all," I called to them in my friendliest tone. "Got enough space for two more up there?"

A narrow-faced girl with dark hair glanced down at me. "Sorry," she said. "We're saving for some friends."

"Oh." My smile wavered as I wondered whether she was telling the truth. Maybe Cassie's cynicism was rubbing off on me.

"Twins!" a voice rang out. "Waters twins! Over here!"

It was Ms. Xavier. She was about halfway down the bleachers in the front row, standing and waving so hard her bangle bracelets were jingling. She gestured to the bench beside her.

"Look, seats!" I told Cassie brightly. Grabbing her wrist, I dragged her along toward Ms. Xavier.

"Hello, girls," the teacher said cheerfully, smoothing out her long skirt. "I'm glad you came. I guess nobody told you that the trick to a good spot for these games is to get here early." She winked and patted the empty bleacher beside her. "But never mind. There's room right here."

"Thanks, Ms. Xavier," I said.

"Yeah, thanks," Cassie muttered, making a point to sit farther away from Ms. X.

Okay, so sitting with a teacher at our first football game wasn't exactly the height of cool. So what?

The play finished with a turnover. One of our players had intercepted a pass and the Armadillos had gained possession of the ball. Everyone around us erupted in cheers and the band blared out a lively fight song. The cheerleaders leaped out onto the sideline and waved their pom-poms. The pounding rhythm of the music filled the stands, and before I knew it, my foot was tapping along with the beat.

Turning, I squinted up toward where the band was sitting a few rows above us. The woodwinds were near the front, and I spotted Bianca right away.

She was dressed in a green-and-gold uniform with an armadillo printed on her shirt, tootling away on her clarinet for all she was worth. When the song ended she lowered her instrument and mopped her brow. I yelled out her name, and she waved back with a smile.

I was still smiling as I turned back to the field, where the cheerleaders were finishing up with a few cartwheels and stuff. Cassie was watching them intently.

"Big surprise," she said. "Megan March is a cheerleader."

Megan was right there in the middle of the squad, jumping and yelling. A few of her friends were there, too, though I didn't see Lavender.

"Yeah, makes sense," I said. "Do you think you'll go out for the squad next year?"

She shot me a look of disbelief. "Are you kidding? As if we'll still be here by then."

"What do you mean?" I asked.

She didn't answer, nodding toward the field. "Next play's starting," she muttered. "We should pay attention."

I turned back toward the action. The Armadillos were actually pretty good. I spotted each of the B Boys out there—Biff and Brent were on the offensive line, while Buzz was a halfback. The fourth B, Brayden, was the quarterback, and I could tell from the first few plays that he was really good. The cheerleaders freaked out and started jumping around every time Brayden moved a muscle.

The game was getting exciting; we were up by four points and I was actually disappointed when the first half ended. "I wonder what the halftime show will be like," I said as the cheerleaders jogged out to the field, doing flips and walkovers on the way.

"Oh, the squad does a marvelous job," Ms. Xavier said. "And our band is one of the best in central Texas."

The visiting team went first, though they'd only brought half a dozen cheerleaders and a small band that marched around haphazardly, playing their fight song. When the home team squad stepped forward, people screamed and cheered and whistled as the cheerleaders danced to a pop song that morphed into our school song at the end. Ms. Xavier sang along loudly, a little off-key, and lots of other people joined in, too, clapping their hands and stomping their feet until the bleachers shook.

"Wow," I whispered to Cassie. "Talk about school spirit!"

"Yeah, I guess." Cass watched as the cheerleaders began to form a pyramid.

The pyramid had three layers already when Megan March stepped forward, doing a quick backflip before climbing up on the other girls' knees. Seconds later she'd scrambled nimbly to the very top. The stands quieted as she carefully caught her balance before standing upright on the other girls' shoulders.

"Go, Armadillos!" she shouted at the top of her lungs, her face red as she yelled again.

She had to be dizzy standing way up there. Strangely, I felt a little dizzy all of a sudden, too. My head swam as I tried to figure out why the scene in front of me looked so familiar. Megan, red-faced and screaming . . .

I gasped as it hit me. She looked like she had in my vision the other day—*exactly* like it! When I closed my eyes, I could still see her bright-red face, her mouth stretched into an emphatic scream. I'd thought it was a scream of pain or terror, which was why I'd been so freaked-out. Now I realized it wasn't that at all. She was just overcome with school spirit!

Clutching the edge of the bleachers, I tried to tell myself it was a coincidence; it had to be. But here she was, exactly as I'd seen her. I'd predicted this moment, just like I'd seen Cassie getting an A on that social studies test. I couldn't believe it.

"Whoa. What's with you?" Cass said. "You look like you ate a bad burrito or something. If you're going to hurl, do it away from me, okay?"

"I—I—" I stammered. I tried to swallow, but my mouth was too dry.

A whistle blew, startling me out of my stupor. I was surprised to see that the cheerleaders were already back on the sideline and our offensive line was on the field. How long did I zone out for? I fixed my gaze on Brayden as he crouched down on the field, ready for the snap.

My sister was still watching me, looking a little worried. "Are you okay? It's pretty hot out here; maybe you should—"

"It's not the heat," I blurted out. "Listen, Cass, something kind of weird has been happening to me lately."

Her gaze drifted back to the field, where the center had snapped the ball to Brayden. Brayden had faked a pass but held on to the ball and was running down the field in our direction, dodging defensive linemen left and right.

"Yeah?" Cass said. "Me, too. I keep having this horrible nightmare that I'm being forced to live in some pathetic little town."

"No, listen, this is for real." I hadn't tried to talk to her about my visions before. What was the point? It wasn't as if we confided in each other anymore. We barely even spoke. But I really needed to talk to someone about what had happened, and no matter how much we'd grown apart, I still knew I could trust her more than anyone else in the world. "Something really weird happened the other day," I told her. "And now something even stranger might have just happened, and I'm not sure, but I think—"

Brayden was still coming closer. He was running right down the sideline, ball tucked into the crook of his arm, head down. A couple of West River players were behind him and losing ground fast, but another one—a big, beefy linebacker—was barreling toward him from the side.

"Oof!"

There was the sickening crunch of helmets and bodies crashing together as the West River player took Brayden down right in front of us. The crowd on the opposite stands whooped, while a sigh of disappointment went up from our side.

Then, a different sound cut through the racket as Brayden rolled over and let out an earsplitting shriek of pain.

7

CASSIE

"BRAYDEN!" I EXCLAIMED as I saw him writhing in agony. Beside me, I heard Cait gasp in shock. I was surprised she'd noticed the tackle, even if it had happened right in front of us, since she'd been babbling on about something pointless. Classic Caitlyn.

As I looked down at Brayden, I didn't stop to think—I just reacted, leaping out of my seat. All around me I could hear people shouting: "What happened?" "I think he's hurt!"

But I ignored them all as I ran to the sideline,

focused on him. Brayden's face was twisted beneath his helmet, his eyes squeezed shut.

"Hold still," I ordered him, grabbing his hand. "You don't want to hurt yourself worse."

What do you know? All those first aid lessons Mom had drummed into us over the years had stuck. I felt weirdly calm and in control.

Brayden gripped my hand so tightly his knuckles went white. "My leg," he moaned.

I glanced at his leg and blanched. It didn't look right—the lower part of the leg was twisting away at an odd angle. Oh, man. This couldn't be good.

The player who'd tackled him was already on his feet, hovering nearby. "He okay?" he asked in a gruff voice. "I didn't hit him that hard, I swear."

"Stay still, okay?" I told Brayden again. "Help will be here soon."

I had no idea if it was true, but Brayden seemed to believe it. His eyes popped open and fixed on me, glazed with fear but focused on my face.

"Th-thanks," he mumbled, squeezing my hand even tighter.

I glanced from his earnest, pain-shrouded hazel eyes to our hands, which were locked together tightly—as if we never wanted to let each other go. . . .

And suddenly my brain jumped to another scene like this. One *exactly* like this.

No way. I had to be making it up. The stress must have affected me, let my imagination run wild. Right? Because it was as if that weirdo-freaky vision I'd had by the water fountain was coming true! Only instead of some romantic hand-holding scene, it was . . . this.

But it couldn't be. I couldn't handle this right now. I'd already lost my home, my friends, and my social standing. I couldn't afford to lose my mind, too.

"Brayden!" A man skidded to his knees on Brayden's other side. "Buddy, you okay?"

"I don't think so, Coach," Brayden burbled. "My leg—it hurts."

I didn't want to stick around to hear any more.

As hard as it was to believe, only a couple of seconds had passed since I'd leaped onto the field. Adults were rushing toward us from every direction, cell phones in hand, shouting questions and instructions. I even heard the jingle of Ms. Xavier's bracelets as she hurried over, announcing that she'd already called 911.

Yanking my hand free, I staggered away, sucking in a few deep breaths and trying to take in what had just happened. I was vaguely aware that Caitlyn was calling my name, though it seemed to be coming from far away. My head spun, and I couldn't seem to stop gulping for air—I knew I needed to get away and calm myself down before I started screaming. Because what I was thinking was impossible. Totally, over-the-top crazy. It couldn't have happened. I was just imagining things; that was all.

Now all I had to do was convince myself of that. . . .

Turning, I shoved my way through the throngs of people flocking toward Brayden. Once I was free

I started to run, desperate to get away. I didn't stop until I reached the restrooms behind the visitor-side bleachers.

I collapsed against the cool, solid concrete wall and slid down to the floor. "Wow," I muttered aloud. "So much for that romantic moment . . ."

I wasn't sure whether to laugh or burst into tears. What had happened back there? It went way beyond déjà vu. Because I knew exactly where I'd seen-felt-*experienced* that moment before.

But how? How could I possibly have seen something that hadn't happened yet? For a second I thought about the other visions I'd had. Had any of them actually come true? I had no idea.

But this one had.

"No way," I said, clenching my fists hard, my nails digging into my palms. "This *so* isn't happening. . . ."

I sat there for a good fifteen minutes or so. My phone kept buzzing in my pocket, but I ignored it.

Finally, when it went off for the twentieth time, I yanked it out and glanced at the screen. It was a text from Cait: **Where are you? We have to talk!**

I wasn't so sure. But I needed to talk to *someone.* We might not be BFFs anymore, but I'd always been able to trust her not to spill my secrets. Besides, she was almost as good as Mom at making me feel better when I was freaking out about something. And now? Yeah, I was definitely freaking out.

I texted back and she arrived minutes later, out of breath and wild-eyed. "Thank goodness!" she cried. "I didn't know what happened to you. Why'd you run off like that?"

"Long story," I said. "How's Brayden?"

She grimaced and flopped down beside me. "They think his leg's broken. The ambulance just got here. It's taking him to the hospital over in Six Oaks. Everyone's totally panicking since Brayden's the quarterback and the home game against the Armadillos' biggest rivals is next Saturday afternoon, and—"

"Cait. Chill," I broke in, recognizing all the signs of a manic Caitlyn monologue. When my sister started talking all fast and excited like that, it was hard to get her to stop.

She blinked at me. "What? I was just saying—"

"I know," I said. "But listen. You said we needed to talk. And you were right. Something weird has been happening."

Suddenly her face went pale. "What do you mean, something weird?"

I peered at her. "Is there something you're not telling me?"

"Is there something *you're* not telling *me*?" she shot back.

I took a deep breath, not quite meeting her eye. "Fine. Lately, I've been . . . seeing things. Like, things that aren't really there."

Pausing, I waited for her to laugh. Look confused. Make fun of me.

But she'd gone completely still. She was staring at me, her eyes as wide as all of Texas.

"Things?" she said after a second. "Like, what kinds of things?"

I shrugged. "Mostly stupid stuff— Wait . . . ?" My own eyes widened, mirroring her, as I got a sudden twitch of that twintuition the two of us used to joke about. "Why are you looking at me like that?"

"Looking at you like what?"

I gasped. "Oh my gosh—it's been happening to you, too!"

8
CAITLYN

MY HEAD WAS spinning. "So you're getting them, too? The visions?"

"Hang on." Cass held up a hand, and I could feel her putting her guard up. "I wouldn't call them 'visions' exactly. It's just that . . . I see weird stuff happening."

My heart was pounding like the snare drum from the marching band. Why hadn't it occurred to me that this could be happening to my twin, too? We'd started off as two halves of the same egg, after all. The two of us had been through everything together, from losing our first baby teeth within a week of each other to getting our tonsils out on the same day.

"So, does it happen when you touch someone?" I asked, leaning forward. "Because that's what seems to trigger it—I mean, not *every* time I touch someone, obviously." I laughed nervously, and it came out sounding excited and breathless. I hadn't realized until that moment how good it would feel to confide in someone.

"Yeah, I guess." Cassie shrugged. "Only once in a while, though; it's happened four or five times, maybe. I can't figure it out."

"Same here. I thought my first vision was just a dream or something. I didn't think it was real. Remember when I had the flu last March?"

As I explained, she nodded. "My first time was sort of random and short and confusing like that, too," she said. "It was at the mall, and I thought I was just super hungry or something. . . ." We went on from there, trading stories of each subsequent vision, each longer, brighter, and more bizarre than the last.

"So, uh, has it happened to you since we moved to Aura?" I asked. I hadn't told her yet about my vision of Megan that first day at the bake sale. To be honest, I was kind of afraid to admit to that one since it would take Cass, oh, about half a second to figure out that it was the reason everyone thought we were weird.

Especially if I told her I'd just seen that particular vision come true.

"Once," she said. "First day of school, when I met Brayden. Nothing too exciting, it was pretty stupid."

All her others had been so detailed—I knew Cassie loved to tell a story—but this time she stopped short. Why wasn't she meeting my eye?

"Okay, then what did you see just now, when you took off like that? Did you have another one?"

"Not exactly." She picked at a stray bit of grass sprouting out of the concrete. "This is going to sound crazy, okay?"

"Crazier than seeing visions?"

"Seriously, Cait. I think—I think I saw Brayden's

accident before it happened. Part of it anyway."

She shot me a sidelong glance, as if expecting me to laugh it off. But I couldn't breathe, and my whole body started shaking. My mind was filled with the image of Megan red-faced and screaming.

"So?" she said sharply. "Are you going to sit there like a dork, or are you going to tell me I'm nuts?"

"You're not nuts," I blurted out. "Or if you are, I guess I am, too. Because the same thing happened to me just now at the game!"

She blinked. "What? You had a vision about Brayden, too?"

"No." I took a deep breath, knowing I *had* to tell her now. "Um, you know how Lavender and those girls have been acting like we have cooties?"

"Gee, I hadn't noticed."

"Well, it's because I sort of bumped into them the first day we got here," I said. "Remember how you ran out of the house? Well, Mom sent me after you, and—"

"I *knew* that's why I ran into you!" Cass exclaimed. "So what happened?"

I told her about the bake sale and the strudel and my bizarre vision of Megan. "So I was all freaked-out, because it looked like she was really scared or hurt or something," I went on. "But when she was on top of the pyramid at halftime, yelling and red from the heat and stuff, it was like total déjà vu." I shrugged. "What I'd seen was happening right there in front of me, but for real this time."

"Wow." Cassie took it all in. "This is totally wacked out. You realize that, right?"

"I guess." I chewed my lower lip, trying to calm myself down. "But listen, it doesn't necessarily have to be a bad thing."

She made a face. "Yeah, right. Now we can get jobs as circus sideshow freaks any time we want."

"No, for real!" My mind was starting to tick as I put it all together. "It's kind of cool, actually. I mean, we can *see the future*! How amazing is that? Maybe we should write down all our visions so far, try to figure out how they work. Maybe more of them might have come true, and—"

"Cait. Stop." Cass frowned. "Seriously. This is so

not a cool little research project or fun party trick, okay? It's weird with a capital W·E·I·R·D. Personally, I'm hoping it's some odd side effect of, like, puberty or air pollution or something. In which case, maybe it'll go away. Like, soon."

"You can't really believe that, can you? Because I don't know about you, but my visions have been getting clearer and longer and more detailed each time. Like, at first I could hardly see what was going on, and now I'm starting to get, you know, details and backgrounds and—"

"Whatever. I don't want to think about it." She climbed to her feet. "At least if it's happening to both of us, I know it's not just me going crazy."

"Are you kidding me?" I exclaimed. "How can you ignore something like this, especially after both of our visions just came true?" I jumped to my feet to face her. "Seriously, Cass—don't you want to know more about how it works? I mean, if we can *see* the future, who knows, maybe we can *change* it, too!" My eyes widened as that thought really sank in. "Like, what if you could have warned Brayden about what you saw? He might have been able to avoid that broken leg!"

Cassie's head snapped around.

"So it's *my* fault Brayden's leg is busted?" she cried. "Really nice, Cait. Thanks a whole freaking lot!"

"No! That's not what I meant at all," I said. "I just—"

"I know, I know. Trying to turn it to the bright side, as usual." She grimaced. "Just give it a rest, okay, Susie Sunshine?"

"Okay. Still, we should probably figure out what to—"

"Another time." She cut me off abruptly. "Right now, I think I'm over football for today. I'm out of here."

"CAIT?" MOM STUCK her head into the hallway. "You almost finished with the hammer?"

"Uh-huh." I tapped the nail I was pounding into the wall one last time and hung up a framed photo of our family. "It's pretty stuffy in here. Can I take a break?"

"Sure." She waved a hand toward the door. "Go outside. Get some fresh air. And while you're out there, maybe you could pull a few weeds. I started the beds along the front walk, but they still need more help."

I forced a smile, then headed for the front door. It was Saturday afternoon, and Mom had been working us hard to get the house in shape.

Outside, Cassie was fiddling with the broken hose faucet. She glanced at me when I stepped onto the stoop but didn't say a word.

That was pretty much how it had been since our talk outside the stadium. But she'd never been that quick to adjust to new things. Maybe I just needed to give her a little more time.

After I spent half an hour pulling weeds, Mom let me take a real break. I went into the bedroom and pulled out my laptop. I'd been searching the web like crazy every chance I got, trying to find anyone else out there who'd had similar visions as me and Cassie. It wasn't easy. There was a ton of information online about stuff like precognition and ESP, but when it came to the personal stories? Well, I don't like to be mean, but a lot of the people posting their experiences seemed not quite right in the head, if you know what I mean.

I was reading an essay by a guy who claimed to have met his future baby in a dream when Cassie walked in. "What are you doing?" she asked.

"Research." I sat up and smiled at her. "Just trying to figure out if we're the only wackos out there who can see the future."

Sometimes humor can snap Cass out of a funk. Today? Not so much.

"Get over it, Caitlyn," she snapped. "Whatever's been happening to us, it has nothing to do with seeing the future. Because that's impossible. Got it?"

Then she spun on her heel and stormed out of the room.

BY THE TIME I walked into school on Monday, I still hadn't found out much more about the visions. It was times like these I wished I had a smartphone, so I could keep scrolling through the sites I found in between classes, but Mama said Cassie and I could get them when we were in high school. Until then, we were stuck with our boring old phones, but I figured I might be able to sneak in some computer time during study hall to look for information. I was sure if I could dig up something concrete, something that sounded legit, I could convince Cassie to take a look. Then maybe we'd know how to handle this new . . . power.

I was heading toward homeroom when I heard loud voices up ahead. Rounding the corner, I saw Liam outside the classroom facing Brent—the blond B Boy—and Lavender Adams. They stood side by side, blocking the doorway.

"Sorry, nerd," Brent said, folding his muscular arms over his chest. "There's a toll to get in now."

"C'mon. Let me go past," Liam said meekly, his head down.

Lavender giggled. "You heard Brent, *Lame-o*," she said. "Pay up."

"Yeah," Brent said with a grin. "Either give us ten bucks now, or hand over your shoes."

"Ew." Lavender wrinkled her nose. "Why would we want Lame-o's stinky shoes?"

Who knew what Brent would have said next, but by then I'd heard enough. Liam was my friend, and in my world friends didn't let friends get picked on by bullies. Stomping over to stand beside Liam, I glared straight at Brent.

"What's wrong with you, you jerk?" I said. My voice came out louder than I'd meant it to. "Nobody elected you two king and queen of homeroom. Let us through!"

Brent blinked, looking surprised. But Lavender kept scowling at me.

"Oh, don't *even* tell me you're in my face again," she said. "Look, we already know you're crazy— both you and your sister."

"That's right, we are. But I'd rather be crazy than be a big old bully like you any day." I took a half step closer. "Better move, or I might sneeze some crazy all over you."

A small crowd was gathering, drawn by the

commotion. Gabe Campbell shoved his way to the front. "Watch out for that one," he said with a sneer, pointing at me. "Her whole family's super shady."

"What?" I shot him an irritated look, still mostly focused on Lavender and Brent.

"You heard me." His eyes narrowed. "You'd better watch yourself, or people in this town might start fighting fire with fire."

"Shut up, Gabe," Lavender snapped. "This so isn't about you."

Gabe shrugged. "That's what you think," he muttered, slinking past Brent into the classroom with one last scowl at me.

"So are you letting us through or not?" I said, taking a step closer to Lavender. "Because I think I feel that cray-cray sneeze coming on."

A few people giggled at that, which got Lavender even more riled up.

"Stay away from me, you freak!" she shouted. "Come on, B. I'm over this."

As she stalked inside, Brent shrugged and followed her. "Later, nerds," he called back over his shoulder.

Liam just stood there, staring at the floor. "You okay?" I asked.

"Yeah, I'm fine. No big deal." His smile was shaky. "Let's just go and sit down, okay?"

I nodded and followed him into class, glancing around the room to make sure there wouldn't be any more trouble. Gabe had his head down and appeared to be fishing for something in his book bag. Brent was clowning around with Biff and Buzz, not noticing us.

But Lavender? She *definitely* noticed. Her eyes bored into me the whole way back to my seat, her stare so cold I almost shivered.

9
CASSIE

WHEN I SIGNED up for art as one of my electives, I thought it might be kind of fun.

That was my first mistake. Because just about anybody could end up in your elective classroom. And I got stuck with Megan. *And* Lavender. *And* two or three of their minions. That's right, the whole stupid little clique.

The worst part? The art teacher, Mrs. Ortega, was at least a hundred years old, half-blind, and more than half-deaf. On my first day of art, she'd assigned us to draw a picture of our favorite food. Then she'd spent the rest of the period at her desk bent over a pile of papers, paying no attention at all to what we were doing. Friday's class? Second verse, same as the first.

That Monday after the football game was my third art class. I was already in a bad mood when I arrived in the studio, as Mrs. Ortega called her classroom. There were two huge, battered old wooden tables with stools all around them.

Every seat at the first table was already taken, while Lavender, Megan, and the minions were parked at one end of the otherwise deserted second table. Great.

I briefly considered dragging a stool over to the first table. But no—I wasn't going to give them the satisfaction of scaring me off. Instead I dropped my bag at the opposite end and sat down.

"Who said you can sit with us?" Lavender called down the table with a smirk.

Megan rolled her eyes. "Don't even talk to her," she advised, without so much as glancing my way. "At least it's this one and not her sister."

For a second I was impressed she could tell Cait and me apart. We didn't dress alike at all, and our hair was different, too. But that had never stopped people from mixing us up.

But then I became seriously annoyed. I could make fun of my sister, sure, but that didn't mean anyone else could.

"What's your problem with my sister anyway?" I demanded. "I mean, get over it already! She dropped some stupid pastry. What's the big deal?"

"It's not even about that anymore." Lavender scowled. "Your twin is such a goody-goody! She'd better watch out, or she's going to make some serious enemies at this school."

I opened my mouth to respond, then closed it. Why was I wasting my energy on these people? I focused on a little Zen chant I'd come up with over the weekend: *Out of here, out of here, out of here . . .*

Because I was more certain than ever that this living-in-Aura thing couldn't last much longer. Mom had kept us busy all weekend—maybe a little *too* busy? Which had led to my latest theory that Mom was working so crazy hard on fixing up the house to take her mind off everything else.

It made perfect sense, right? I mean, she hadn't said much about her new job so far, except that this was probably the last weekend she'd have off for a while. Maybe she was already hating the job, regretting this move, realizing she'd made a ginormous mistake. I wouldn't be surprised at all. It might be hard for Cait and me to adjust to living here, but it couldn't be easy for Mom either, right? I'd seen enough movies and TV shows about small towns to know how things usually went when a city mouse tried to fit in with the locals. When Mom ran out of home improvement projects to distract her, would she finally admit that this place was never going to feel like home—and start thinking about moving us back to San Antonio?

I crossed my fingers under the art room table. With any luck, maybe I'd only have to survive this place for another week or two. I might be back in San Antonio in time to celebrate my twelfth birthday next month with my friends!

And with a little extra luck, my wacky new visions would go away, too. Then my life could go back to normal. I crossed the fingers on my other hand and smiled, almost able to *taste* how that would feel. . . .

There was a commotion by the door, and I glanced over in time to see Brayden holding on to the doorframe with his left hand. He'd shown up that morning on crutches, his lower leg encased in a cast. One of his crutches was under his right arm, and the other had fallen to the floor.

"Oops," he said with a sheepish grin. "Guess I'm not used to these things yet." Still clinging to the doorframe, he waved his crutch.

"Did you drop one, Brayden? I'll get it for you!" Lavender hopped out of her seat and scurried over.

I watched out of the corner of my eye, pretending to be busy searching for something in my bag. Lavender retrieved the crutch from the doorway and carefully slid it under Brayden's arm.

"Thanks, Lav," he said. Hobbling into the room, he lowered himself carefully onto a seat at our table.

He glanced over at me.

"Hey, Cassie," he said with a smile. "What's up?"

"Not much," I replied automatically, carefully keeping my focus on my bag.

I couldn't let him see my face. Because when he'd looked at me, a really weird combination of guilt and curiosity had started swirling through my mind. What if Cait was right? What if I *could* have saved him from that crash?

But no—I cut off the thought. It wasn't my fault. Until that terrible moment at the game, I hadn't even known those stupid visions *could* come true! *If* that was even what had happened. And how was I supposed to guess a seemingly nice image of holding hands would turn into a broken leg anyway? Talk about random!

Speaking of random stuff, I was sure the visions would go away as randomly as they'd come. At least I hoped so. It was hard enough trying to feel normal in Awful Aura without that freaky-deaky business hanging over my head.

"Okay," Brayden said. "So, uh, anyway, thanks

for helping me the other day. You know, at the game?"

"Oh!" I glanced up at him quickly, feeling my face go hot. Could he see that? "Um, it was no biggie. You know—I was there. Anyone would've done the same thing."

He smiled uncertainly. "Yeah. Well, anyway, I really—"

"Brayden!" Lavender interrupted loudly. "Do you have a pen I can borrow?"

He turned away. "Sure, probably," he said, digging into his pocket.

Ignoring the smug look of triumph Lavender shot my way, I slumped on my stool and stared at the table. *Forget about him, girl,* I told myself. *It doesn't matter. Brayden's cute, but this whole Aura thing is temporary. Out of here, remember?*

"PERFECT TIMING!" CAIT sang out from the kitchen as Mom came in the front door that evening. "Dinner will be ready in ten minutes."

I looked up from the sofa where I was flipping through my math book. Mom was in her uniform, and she looked more stressed-out than usual. Was there that much crime to deal with in a tiny town like Aura? Or were the locals turning out to be difficult to deal with, like I'd been thinking earlier? Either way, good. Maybe that would help convince her to take us back to nice, safe San Antonio.

"Thanks, girls," Mom said, kicking off her shoes. "That gives me enough time to hop in the shower and wash off my day."

She disappeared down the narrow hall, and a moment later came the sound of the water handle creaking on. In a house that small, we had no secrets. I listened for the loud gospel singing that usually accompanied Mom's showers, but all I heard was the water running.

Finally Cait glanced over from the stove, where she was stirring soup. "Mom looks pretty tired, don't you think?"

"Yeah," I said. "Maybe the new job's turning out to be more than she can handle."

Cait looked down into the soup pot. "Doubtful. Mom can handle anything." But she didn't sound so sure. She shot an uneasy glance in the direction of the bathroom.

Hmm. Maybe this was my chance. What if Cait was beginning to think the same way I was? If we teamed up, it might be easier to convince Mom to admit she'd made a mistake by bringing us here.

"Listen, Cait," I said, dropping my book on the sofa and stepping into the kitchen. I leaned against the chipped countertop, watching my sister stir. "Do you get the feeling she's not that into being here?"

Cait rolled her eyes. "I get the feeling *you're* not that into it. Mom seems fine."

"Really?" I pursed my lips. "Maybe you should start paying more attention. Because I think she's already regretting the move."

"What makes you say that?" Cait kept her eyes on the soup.

"Lots of little hints." I shrugged. "The point is, you probably shouldn't get too comfortable at Aura Middle School, or with your geeky new friends. Because I can tell Mom's not happy. I have a strong feeling we'll be back in San Antonio in time to go to the Holiday River Parade in November."

"You do, hmmmm?"

Uh-oh. That wasn't Cait. It was Mom.

I spun around to face her. She'd come into the kitchen without me hearing, padding along on bare feet. She stared at me sternly, wrapped in her favorite red-flowered kimono robe, with one eyebrow cocked.

"Oh, hi, Mom. Didn't hear you there," I said weakly. "I was just saying . . ."

"I heard what you were *just* saying, Cassandra," Mom said, her voice like iron. "And I'm telling you to knock it off."

"But—"

"No. You need to listen." The scarymama voice was back. "We're in Aura to stay, and there's zero chance we're moving back, so you'd better get used to it. Both of you." Mom expanded her glare to include Caitlyn for a second before focusing her laser eyes back on me. "My new job is going fine so far. It's a big adjustment, of course, like I know that moving here is an adjustment for you two."

"But—" I tried again.

"*But*," Mom cut me off, "I fully intend to work hard to fit in with the force here and make a career out of it. I suggest you do the same at school." Then her expression softened. "I do hope you'll make an effort to be happy here, girls. Aura is our home now. And I know it can be a good place for all of us."

She held my gaze steadily, and I tried to find a smidgen of doubt in her deep-brown eyes.

Nothing. Could she really mean what she was telling me? Was I really stuck here—forever?

Caitlyn cleared her throat. "Um, the soup's ready," she said softly.

"Good." Mom finally broke my gaze, turning to sniff at the steam rising from the pot. "Smells great; I'm famished."

"Not me," I muttered, backing out of the kitchen. "In fact, I've totally lost my appetite. Think I'll go finish my homework."

"Stop right there," Mom ordered. "Homework can wait. We're eating dinner as a family—all three of us."

I was tempted to argue, but what was the point? I felt grown-up, but in the eyes of the world I was still a kid, which meant I had no rights. And apparently no voice, even in my own family. So I took my seat at the tiny table without another word, trying to ignore the way my chair wobbled on the uneven floor and the faint smell of burned food that still lingered even after scrubbing the whole house from top to bottom.

Mom could force me to sit down for dinner. She could even force me to live here in Aura.

But she couldn't force me to like it.

THAT NIGHT I tossed and turned long after Cait had fallen asleep, trying to figure out what to do. My mind skittered around like a nervous cat, unable to settle on any solution to the problem my life had become, any plan to get me out of here.

But somewhere around midnight I finally had to admit it—I was stuck. I wouldn't be back home for my birthday after all. Or for Thanksgiving, or even Christmas. Mom had made up her mind, and she could be even more stubborn than I was. Which meant I was going to be forced to stay here.

The thought made me want to cry. But no. I wasn't going to let Aura beat me. If this was my life now, I'd just have to figure out how to make it work.

At that moment Cait let out a soft groan and turned over. I glanced across the tiny room, squinting in the dim light leaking in from the streetlamps. If only my sister hadn't made such a mess of things by getting herself on the outs with the in crowd before we had even unpacked one box. Because as obnoxious as Lavender could be, she was undeniably popular. And Megan and the others actually seemed pretty cool in most ways—you know, other than the making-my-life-miserable part. And that wasn't so much their fault as Cait's, right? I mean, I probably would have acted the same way toward a new kid who did something so freaky right off the bat.

I lay back and stared up at the shadows dancing on the ceiling. There had to be a way to restore my social status. That would make life in Aura a little better. I'd have cool friends again; I wouldn't have to watch my back every second of the day; maybe I'd even be able to get to know Brayden better. . . .

Brayden. That was the silver lining to all this, right?

And thinking about Brayden made me think about something else. Could I really have stopped him from breaking his leg if I'd figured out my vision in time? Cait seemed to think we could use our visions to change the future, to make things better.

And what would be better than using this power to become popular?

10
CAITLYN

"WANT TO PLAY a game?" Liam asked as we walked into the school library for study hall Tuesday afternoon. He grinned, flicking his hair off his forehead. "I know how to unblock games on the school computers."

"Can't," Bianca said. "I need to do research for my social studies project." She wandered off toward the stacks without waiting for a response.

"Caitlyn? How about you?" Liam looked at me hopefully.

I didn't answer. Gabe had just stalked into the library. He glanced around, his cold eyes settling on me. I swallowed hard as he headed our way.

"Hey," he said, his voice gruff. "You live in that junky little place on Granite Street, right?"

"Why are you asking?" I said cautiously.

His eyes narrowed. "Just making conversation," he snapped. "Anyway, you don't have to answer. I have ways of finding stuff out, okay? My family's lived in this town forever. We belong here, and it doesn't pay to cross us. Don't forget that."

He spun on his boot heel and hurried off. I watched him go, feeling troubled. With everything else that had been going on, I'd almost forgotten about Gabe's weird comments that first day.

"I still don't know why he thinks my mom stole his uncle's job," I said to Liam. "I want to ask Mom, but Cassie's been giving her fits lately, and, well, I kind of don't want to get into it."

"Yeah," Liam said sympathetically. "All I know is his uncle was a cop for years. But he retired a couple of months ago."

"So he's old?"

"Not really. He's younger than my parents, I think."

"Why'd he retire, then?" I asked.

Liam shrugged. "Something about his family? There was an article on the town website, but I didn't really read it. I can pull it up for you if you want."

"Sure." I dropped my schoolbag on the table next to a free computer terminal. "Thanks."

Within seconds I was scanning the article. It was only about six lines long, mentioning Charles Campbell's years of distinguished service as an officer of the law as well as his earlier status as a high school football hero.

"'We wish Mr. Campbell the best of luck as he takes this opportunity to spend more time with his family,'" I read aloud. That was it—the article ended there. "Hmm. Not very specific."

"Yeah." Liam didn't seem too interested. "So what do you say? Want to play a game?"

"Rain check?" I said, still staring at the article.

It hadn't told me much. Oh, well—Gabe wasn't my biggest problem right now, so I did my best to forget about him. "I wanted to research something today, too, actually," I told Liam.

"Oh." He looked slightly disappointed. "You don't really have to start your social studies project yet, you know. Bianca always does all her homework as early as she can. She can't help herself."

"It's not that." I hesitated, not sure how much to tell him. Liam already felt like a true friend, but that didn't mean I was ready to confide in him about my visions just yet. Besides, now that Cassie was involved, it wouldn't feel right to spill our secret without asking her first. But I had to tell him *something*. Normally I didn't like lying, especially to friends. But what else could I do under the circumstances? So I thought fast.

"It's more for, uh, personal interest," I said. "I saw something on TV about people with, like, extrasensory powers and stuff? I wanted to look into it more, you know, see how much of it's for real."

My cheeks were flaming, and I was sure my eyes

looked shifty. Luckily Liam didn't seem to notice. In fact, his face lit up with interest.

"Fascinating!" he exclaimed. "I've done a little reading on that subject myself, off and on. I'll help if you want."

"Sure, thanks." I closed the newspaper article, then pushed the mouse toward Liam.

"What kind of psi powers are you interested in?" Liam prompted. "Like, ESP or telekinesis or what?"

"How about, um, seeing the future?" Even saying it out loud felt dangerous, like he might guess my secret.

He nudged my hands off the keyboard and took over, typing fast. "That's called precognition," he said as he typed. "There've actually been tons of studies about that."

"Really?" I was surprised. "What kinds of studies?"

"You know." He shrugged, grabbing the mouse. "Trying to prove whether it really happens. See?"

I glanced at the screen. He'd pulled up a site about learning to predict the future through your dreams.

"Oh," I said. "Does that kind of thing only happen in dreams, or can it happen when people are awake, too?"

"Sure, either way, I think." He clicked off the dream page and picked another entry from the search engine. "Here's one about waking premonitions. . . ."

For the rest of the class period, I read all kinds of sites about precognition and similar stuff. Some of them seemed almost scientific, while others were kind of out there. But none quite seemed to match what had been happening to me and Cass.

As I was scanning a parapsychology message board, Bianca came over to ask Liam for help with something. He hurried off with her just as I found an entry with an intriguing title:

"Real Psychics in the UK? A Vision of the Future"

I opened the thread and scanned it. It started off talking about some British family called the Lockwoods and a bunch of stuff about the history of England, and I almost clicked away. Then the phrase "waking visions prompted by touch" caught my eye, and I froze.

I scanned the rest of the entry. There wasn't much more than that—whoever had posted it claimed to have found an old diary in a secondhand shop. It was written by some guy named Lockwood who supposedly saw visions of people's futures when he touched them. Lockwood had developed this power suddenly, around the time of his twelfth birthday.

My heart pounded as I read it over again. I scrolled down through the responses to the original post, but most of them only said stuff like "Interesting!" or "Sounds cool" or "I'm way past 12, guess I won't be getting that power! LOL!"

I read the original post again. This was the first real story I'd found that sounded exactly like what was happening to us! Even down to the twelfth birthday—ours was right around the corner. How could I find out more?

Out of the corner of my eye, I could see Liam wandering in my direction. Scanning the thread again, I noticed that the posters all had screen names like PsychicGuy42 or CuriousInCali. Right—the internet could be an anonymous place. Maybe the perfect kind of place to ask for help without giving away my secret. . . . I clicked open a text box and typed fast:

Does anyone know more about this kind of precognition? I think my twin sis and I might have the same thing. We're almost 12 and we've been experiencing something similar. But we're not in the UK; we're in the US. Please message me with more info!

I read it over one more time and posted it, signing it VisionTwin01.

By the time Liam reached me, I'd closed the site. "Almost time for the bell," he said cheerfully. "Did you get enough info?"

"Yeah," I said, logging off. "Let's go."

MOM GOT HOME at the same time Cass and I did that day. By the time Mom had changed out of her uniform, Cassie had disappeared into our bedroom, claiming to be super busy with some tough math problems. I was skeptical—since when did Cass have trouble with math?—but Mom bought it. Or maybe she just didn't want to fight with Cassie anymore, especially after the confrontation they'd had the night before.

Me? Apparently I was fair game.

"We need to get the floor sanded down here by the door," Mom said, waving a hand at the wooden floorboards in the entryway. "See? It's all stained from foot traffic, so it doesn't match the back hallway."

"What do you want me to do?" I asked.

Mom grabbed her purse off the bench by the door. "I picked up some new sandpaper for the sander," she said. She started shuffling through the bag, pulling out a huge ring of keys and setting it on the bench, followed by a pair of sunglasses and a pack of gum. Finally, she fished out a package of sandpaper. Tossing the purse next to everything she'd just pulled out of it, she hurried off to fetch the belt sander.

Soon I was on my knees trying to keep the vibration of the sander from rattling my teeth too much. The mindless work gave me time to think.

Would anybody respond to my message online?

I'd checked my in-box right after school, but there had been nothing yet. It was probably a long shot, especially since that original post had been written a couple of months ago. But it was the only shot I had so far. . . .

A loud knock on the door jolted me out of my thoughts. Clicking off the sander, I stood and stepped over to open the door. I was shocked to find Gabe Campbell standing there—greasy hair, cowboy boots, and all. He was holding a brown paper bag.

"Hey," he said. "Caitlyn, right? Not the other one?" He peered at me.

"Yeah, it's Caitlyn." I was too surprised to say anything else. It was weird to see him outside of school, sort of like running into your dentist at the mall or something. The bigger surprise? He almost seemed, well, *nice*. At least compared to the way he'd acted at the library that day. And every other time I'd seen him, pretty much.

"I'm selling raffle tickets for a free car wash," Gabe went on, holding up the paper bag. "You know, for the class trip fund-raiser? Is your mom home?"

He stepped forward into the doorway, looking around inside the house. Yeah, he was being polite and all, but I couldn't help but think his expression was a little shifty. I took a step back out of his way, feeling nervous.

Snap out of it, girl, I told myself. *This is obviously why he was asking where you lived!*

The thought made me feel better. Since when did I think bad stuff about people who weren't doing anything wrong? Maybe Cass's suspicious nature was rubbing off on me.

"Mom's in the backyard," I told Gabe. "Wait here and I'll go get her."

"Sure." He stepped into the entryway and sat down on the bench, nudging Mom's purse and all the other stuff out of his way.

I hesitated for one more moment, glancing at Mom's purse with her wallet tucked inside. What if . . . No. I wasn't going there.

"Be right back," I said, hurrying toward the back hallway.

Five minutes later, Mom was digging into her purse for money to pay for a raffle ticket. I held my breath, relieved when she opened her wallet and I could see the cash inside. Immediately I felt foolish for doubting Gabe's intentions.

"Thank you so much, Ms. Waters," he said, sticking out his hand to shake after he'd traded the raffle ticket for the money my mom donated. "We really appreciate your support."

"Of course." Mom smiled at him. "Good luck selling all the tickets."

"Thanks." After he shook Mom's hand, Gabe reached over to shake mine, too. I took it cautiously. His palm felt warm and oddly sticky, but I didn't have much time to think as a piercing, buzzing sound started inside my head, ringing through my brain. Suddenly, Gabe began to shimmer in front of my eyes.

Oh, no! It was happening again. . . .

There were two versions of Gabe standing before me now. A faded-out Gabe was politely shaking my hand. The other, much brighter Gabe was also smiling, but it was a big, triumphant grin. Suddenly I noticed that the view behind him had changed, too. Instead of the quiet street outside my house, I saw the Aura police station. A middle-aged man I didn't recognize was there, too, wearing a blue shirt and a shifty-eyed look. Gabe was handing the man something, though I couldn't quite see what it was.

Gabe yanked his hand away from mine fast, and his vibrant double disappeared. Mom was still busy tucking her raffle ticket into her wallet, but Gabe was looking at me funny now.

"Uh, see you at school tomorrow," he muttered warily.

"Yeah," I managed to choke out. "See you."

"What a nice young man," Mom said after she'd closed the door behind him. She bent to scoop the keys and other stuff back into her purse. "Is he in your class at school?"

"Uh-huh," I said, relieved when Mom headed back outside.

I sank onto the bench, shaking from head to toe. This had been my most vivid vision yet—and they were definitely getting stronger. I mean, I'd never noticed the scenery before! What did it mean? I had to tell Cass what had happened!

But she'd been awfully quiet since the thing at dinner last night, and Bad-Mood Cass was never easy to deal with. I could only hope she'd get over herself soon. Because whatever was happening to us was getting more intense by the day, and I needed my sister right now, for real. More than I could remember needing her since we were little kids.

So I grabbed the sander and went back to work, trying to ignore how lonely her silence made me feel.

11
CASSIE

"LISTEN," CAITLYN SAID, skipping over a crack in the sidewalk. "I can't wait any longer to tell you or I'll go nuts!"

It was Wednesday morning, and we were halfway to school. Cait had been quiet for the first part of the walk, but then it was like a dam had burst, and she'd suddenly started chattering nonstop. Definitely *not* what I needed on an important day like today—a day that could make or break my entire school career in Aura.

"I had another vision yesterday."

Well, *that* got my attention. Her voice was slightly louder than your average foghorn. My sister was seriously lacking in the art of cool.

"Sssh!" I warned, my eyes darting around to see who might have heard. Now that I had a plan to become popular, I didn't want my sister to blow it for me. Again. "Can we talk about this later? And, you know, *not* in public?"

"Oh." Her face fell. "Sure, I guess."

As we approached school, I ran my hands over my outfit, making sure everything was where it should be. I'd taken extra time getting ready that morning, ignoring Cait's increasingly frantic pounding on the bathroom door. Super stylish outfit? Check. Perfect hair? Check. Cute lip gloss (the only makeup Mom let us wear)? Check.

I looked the part. Now it was time to put my plan into action.

Normally I headed straight to homeroom after hitting my locker. Not today. I wandered the halls, keeping an eye out for members of the popular crowd.

The first one I found was one of the minions. She was a petite strawberry blonde named Emily. She was at her locker, touching up her lip gloss in a tiny mirror taped inside the door.

"Hey, girl," I said, stepping up to her. "Listen, do you know, uh, which chapters we were supposed to read for English today?"

As I said it, I put a hand on her arm. You know, casual-like. She glanced at me, then at my hand, looking confused.

"Why are you talking to me?" she said, capping her gloss.

I stood still and focused on Emily's face intently, waiting for the buzzing sound and the rest. But nothing happened. Why wasn't anything happening? A second later Emily shrugged off my hand.

"Why are you *touching* me, weirdo?" she said. "Get away."

I slumped against the lockers as she hurried off, shooting a couple of suspicious looks back at me as she went. Okay, so that had been a bust.

But before I could worry about it, I spotted a

couple of the B Boys coming down the hall. They weren't in my section, but I knew who they were. *Everybody* knew who they were.

"Hey, guys," I said, stepping out to block their path. "What's up?"

The shorter B Boy, Biff, blinked at me. "Caitlyn?"

"Nah, it's the other one, bro," the second guy said, rubbing his short black hair, which I guessed was the reason everyone called him Buzz. "Twins, remember?"

"Oh, right. Yo, what's happening, other twin?" Biff looked me up and down.

I leaned closer, touching his arm. "Not much. You guys ready for the game this weekend?" Everyone had been talking about the upcoming game against Jeffers Middle School, Aura's biggest rival. The entire school—actually the entire *town*—was freaking out about it, practically nonstop.

"Dude! For sure!" Biff turned and high-fived Buzz.

My hand dropped away, and I lost contact.

I bit my lip, frustrated. I was getting nothing.

Again. Why wasn't this working?

Then again, it wasn't like I got a vision *every* time I touched someone. So how could I make it happen now?

"You coming to watch us kick some butt?" Buzz asked with a big grin, holding up his hand.

"Oh. Uh, yeah, sure. Of course," I said, high-fiving him.

And just as my hand met his, my hearing and vision shorted out. Even in that brief second I caught a clear glimpse of a second, extravivid Buzz layered over the real one. He was scowling down at a test paper with a big, red D scribbled at the top.

Great. How was I supposed to use something like that? Telling Buzz to study harder wasn't likely to win me any popularity points.

"Gotta go," I muttered to the jocks, darting past them and striding down the hall.

I needed to make this work. I had to, if I was going to survive Aura. But I couldn't just go around randomly touching people, or—

"Oof!" I grunted as I rounded the corner and

slammed right into someone. Oops. I really had to stop doing that.

"Oh!" my victim blurted out.

It was Liam, Cait's geeky friend. He wobbled, and I automatically grabbed his arm to steady him.

Another vision hit me hard and fast. Suddenly wobbly hallway Liam dimmed behind another Liam, this one standing in the lunch line.

Whoa! As I watched, lunchroom Liam got bumped badly by Brent, who was behind him in line. Liam lurched forward, scraping against the corner of the metal tray return. He straightened up quickly, glancing down at himself with alarm. His pants had caught on the metal edge and ripped, gaping open, to reveal superhero underpants underneath. Lunchroom Liam quickly pulled off his sweater and wrapped it around his waist, face flaming. . . .

"Cassie! Cassie? Are you okay?"

I floated back to reality as Liam—the real one—pulled his arm away and waved a hand in front of my face. Blinking at him, I took a step back.

"Uh, sorry," I muttered, trying not to smirk at

the thought of those goofy undies. "You must've half-knocked me out, crashing into me like that."

"Oh! Sorry. Do you want me to walk you to the school nurse?"

"No, it's cool." I said, and hurried off without another word.

For a second I was annoyed. Here I was trying so hard to make a vision happen, and when it finally did, it was a total waste! And of course my vision of Liam would be something lame like ripping his pants and showing his dorky underwear. No wonder all the cool kids thought he was a nerd. Which meant they thought the same thing about my sister, his new BFF. If my vision came true, I could only imagine how their increased nerditude might rub off on me.

Or wait. Maybe this vision wasn't all bad news after all. In fact, maybe it was exactly what I'd been looking for. . . .

I LOITERED IN the hall outside homeroom, trying to look casual. Just as I was starting to wonder if Megan had cut school that day, she finally appeared.

For once she was alone, no minions in sight. Good. That might make this easier.

"Hey, Megan," I said as she approached, trying to sound nonchalant. "How's it going?"

She looked startled. Her pale brows knit together, and I braced myself for an insult. Instead she just said, "Hey. Cool boots."

"Thanks." I mentally patted myself on the back for that day's choice in footwear. "I like your skirt."

Megan looked great, as always. Her style was a little girlier and more pastel-y than mine, but the girl knew how to dress. Even if I didn't need her to become popular, that would be enough reason to want to be her friend.

"So listen," I said quickly. "I heard something funny might happen at lunch today."

"Something funny?" she echoed cautiously. "What do you mean?"

I psyched myself up and pasted what I hoped was a cool, slightly mischievous grin on my face. "It's a surprise. But trust me; you won't want to miss it. Meet me by the lunch line if you want to see."

Megan didn't answer right away. I held my breath, trying to look as if I didn't care that much about her response. Her cool-blue eyes flicked down to my boots again, then back to my face.

"Maybe," she said. "We'd better get inside. The bell's about to ring."

She brushed past me into homeroom, and I let out my breath. Whew! I could tell she wasn't going to cut me much slack. This might be my one chance to win her over.

But that was okay. One chance was all I needed.

"SO WHEN'S THIS thing going to happen?"

Megan sounded impatient. We were hovering near the tray return, and though kids kept filing past us, Liam hadn't shown yet.

"Soon," I assured Megan, trying to sound confident. "Any minute now."

A burst of laughter came from nearby. I'd recognize that goofy, too-loud guffaw anywhere—it was Cait. Glancing over, I saw her hurrying toward the line with Liam and Bianca.

My heart pounded. This was it!

"Heads up," I said quietly, nudging Megan with my shoulder. "Eyes on the nerd."

"You mean Liam?" Megan frowned, looking confused.

"Hi, Cass," Caitlyn said cheerfully as they passed us. "Why aren't you in line?"

"Hi," I said, not bothering to answer.

Luckily she didn't seem to care. She grabbed a tray, and Liam waved her and Bianca ahead of him in line.

I glanced around. When was Brent going to show? I couldn't see him anywhere. And trust me, he was easy to spot—he towered over most of the other students, and his white-blond spiked hair added at least another inch. Not exactly a guy who blended in with the crowd.

"Where's Brent?" I asked Megan.

"Brent?" She shrugged. "He's out today. I heard he ditched to go look at a car with his cousin."

I froze, my whole body going hot and cold both at once. No. This couldn't be happening. Then I noticed that Liam was wearing a T-shirt instead of the striped polo and cardigan sweater from my vision.

Duh! How could I have been so stupid? It had taken days for my vision about Brayden to come true. Why had I assumed this latest vision would occur today?

"Yo, ladies!" Suddenly Biff bounded up behind us with Buzz at his heels. "Out of our way—we're starving!"

"Yeah." Buzz patted his stomach. "We gotta keep our strength up for Saturday's game; know what I mean?"

Lavender was right behind the guys. She zeroed in on Megan and me standing together, and her face got all pinched and suspicious. "Megan, what are you doing?" she said sharply. "Get away from that freak, or you'll get crazy cooties."

Oh, man. I was about to give up—on my plan, on befriending Megan, on ever having a life again. I'd blown it. And even if the vision I'd seen happened tomorrow or a week from now, there was no way

Megan would ever give me a chance again. No. Way.
I was doomed. I might as well buy some Wonder
Woman underpants and start hanging out with my
sister and the Dork Patrol.

Just then Liam let out a loud, snorty burst of
laughter, and I winced. No—I couldn't give up yet.

A new idea hit me. Maybe my vision wasn't
meant for today. But that didn't mean I couldn't use
what I'd seen. Crossing my fingers, I pasted a cool
smile on my face.

"Hang on," I told Megan. "Here we go."

I glanced at Liam, who was still laughing. For a
second I hesitated. The poor guy had enough problems without this, didn't he?

Then I saw Megan watching me with narrowed
eyes. I took a deep breath. *Sorry, dude,* I thought in
Liam's direction. *No sense both of us being outcasts . . .*

Grabbing Biff by the arm, I pulled him toward
me, whispering in his ear. He listened, and his face
lit up with glee.

Biff casually sauntered up to where Liam was

bent over the counter examining the choices in Jell-O flavors.

In one swift movement, Biff grabbed the waistband of Liam's corduroys, yanking downward. The pants came down—revealing a pair of superhero briefs.

As the other kids howled with laughter, I blew out a slow sigh of relief. Just as I'd guessed, Liam had a whole collection of those undies. Today's pair wasn't quite as colorful as the ones in my vision, but they would do.

"Come on, Cassie." Megan linked her arm through mine and smiled at me. "Why don't you sit with us today?"

I glanced at Liam, feeling a twinge of guilt. But I shook it off and smiled back at Megan.

Yes, they would do quite nicely.

12

CAITLYN

"WHERE HAVE YOU been?" I blurted out as soon as Cassie walked through the front door.

I'd been waiting for her ever since I got home from school. I'd checked my email—still no response from that message board post—and was trying to start my homework.

Trying being the key word. I hadn't been able to concentrate, mostly because I was too busy convincing myself not to jump to conclusions about what had happened at lunch. I really, really-for-real wanted to give my twin the benefit of the doubt.

There was just one problem. My twintuition was kicking in again. And it was giving me the sneaking suspicion that Cassie might have had something to do with the pantsing incident. I narrowed my eyes at her, hoping I was wrong.

"Check it out." Cass dropped the shopping bag she was carrying on the bench by the door. Reaching inside, she pulled out a blouse. "What do you know? You can find a few cute things out here in the boonies after all—if you're shopping with someone who knows where to look."

She pranced over and waggled the shirt in front of me, but I batted it aside. "Who were you shopping with?" I demanded, already knowing the answer.

"Oh, you know, Megan and Lav and a couple of the other girls," Cassie replied airily, stepping away and tossing her new blouse back in the bag. "Megan's older sister is home from college this week, so she drove us to the mall over in Six Oaks."

"Since when are you friends with Megan and Lavender?" I wanted to stay calm, but I couldn't do it. Leaping off the sofa, I got in her face. "Did it maybe have something to do with the way y'all totally humiliated Liam today in front of the entire school?"

"What?" She stepped back, her eyes wide. "I don't know what you're talking about."

"Yes, you do." I gritted my teeth. "Admit it, okay? You put that jock up to it, didn't you?"

"You mean the thing with Captain Underpants? I was an innocent bystander." She pursed her lips, clearly trying not to laugh. "I mean, it's one thing to get pantsed. But really, who could *possibly* have predicted he'd have something like *that* on underneath, right?"

I stared at her. Who *was* this person? What had happened to my sister? "Liam was really upset," I said softly. "He didn't say much, but I could tell."

"Then maybe he should wear normal underwear." Grabbing her shopping bag, Cassie swept past me and disappeared down the hall. A second later I heard our bedroom door slam.

I slumped down on the sofa. Okay, so she hadn't

come out and admitted having anything to do with what had happened. And I preferred to give people the benefit of the doubt—especially my own sister.

But it was a pretty big coincidence, wasn't it? On the very day the popular kids decided to mess with Liam, Cassie became best friends with them out of nowhere. She'd been popular at pretty much every school we'd ever attended, especially the one in San Antonio. How far would she go to be in the in crowd here? I had no idea, and it scared me a little—suddenly I felt like I didn't know my own other half anymore.

THE NEXT DAY at lunch I barely heard a word Liam and Bianca said. I had a perfect view of the table in the middle of the cafeteria where the cool kids always sat. And today Cassie was right there in the center of the action. She was chatting and laughing and waving her French fries around, clearly having a great time with her new friends.

I bit my lip as I watched her playfully bump shoulders with Megan. Maybe I was reading too much into this whole situation. Maybe it all really was a coincidence. Maybe I should be happy that my twin was finally settling in.

"Come on, Liam!" Bianca's voice broke into my thoughts. "I'm freezing, and you're obviously not."

Bianca was hugging herself and glaring at Liam as he looked down at his lunch, his expression sort of angsty.

"Sorry," he muttered, still not meeting Bianca's eye. "I need to keep it, that's all."

"What's wrong?" I asked Bianca.

She turned to me with a frown. "Liam won't let me borrow his sweater," she complained.

Liam's bright-red sweater, which clashed pretty dramatically with his brown-and-green-striped polo shirt, was tied firmly around his waist.

"Here, you can borrow mine," I told Bianca, fishing out the cardigan I'd tossed in my bag that morning. "I don't need it."

"Thanks!" Bianca accepted the sweater, immediately looking much happier. "I'll give it back as soon as I can get mine out of my locker."

"No hurry." I smiled distractedly, my gaze already wandering back toward my sister.

As we left the cafeteria a few minutes later, Liam grabbed my arm, holding me back.

"Thanks, Caitlyn," he said quietly, sounding unusually serious. "You know—for the sweater thing?"

"Sure, no biggie."

"No, really." He glanced around to make sure nobody was looking our way. "See, I didn't want to tell Bianca where other people might hear me— you know, after yesterday and all. But I, uh, tripped and ripped my pants in the lunch line." He tweaked the sweater aside just enough for me to see a hint of Superman peeking out through a tear in his khakis. "I couldn't be a laughingstock two days in a row."

"Oh!" Now I understood. Talk about bad luck!

Or was it? Suddenly something else was starting to make perfect sense, too. Horrible, awful sense.

As Liam hurried to catch up with Bianca, I stood there in shock. Cassie's words from yesterday started running through my mind in an endless loop: *Who could* possibly *have predicted he'd have something like that on underneath?*

My twintuition had been right! Cassie must have had a vision about Liam ripping his pants and decided to use his, um, unusual fashion sense to win over her snooty new friends.

"How dare she!" I whispered.

It took a lot to make me mad, but right now I was ready to chew metal and spit nails. How could Cassie have done something like this? What had Liam ever done to her? I wanted to find her and give her a piece of my mind.

But I forced myself to take a few deep breaths. Getting mad at Cassie never got me anywhere. She had what she wanted now—popularity—and no amount of yelling and ranting from me was likely to get through to her. This wasn't the time to get mad. It was time to get even.

After all, two could play at this game.

13

CASSIE

THE NEXT MORNING I must have tried on every out-fit I owned, struggling to decide what to wear. It was Friday, and now that things were going so well with Megan and the gang, I was fixing to get myself invited to their weekend plans.

Well, it was *mostly* going well anyway. Megan was already starting to feel like a real friend. We actually had a ton in common: we liked a lot of the same stuff, from fashion to movies, and we laughed at each other's jokes. Most of the minions seemed to accept me, too. If Megan thought I was cool, that was good enough for them.

Then there was Lavender. She was going to be a tough case, I could tell. Oh, she didn't exactly say or do anything wrong or mean or whatever. But she didn't exactly act super friendly either. She mostly avoided me, and I caught her watching me with narrowed eyes more than a few times.

I wasn't too worried, though. All I needed was to find something to bond over with her, and we'd be good. But first we needed to spend more quality time together. Starting this weekend, I hoped.

The weather had taken a turn toward the less-than-stifling over the past couple of days, so I pulled a striped cardigan from the bottom of a drawer and held it up, surveying myself in the mirror.

"That one's cute," Caitlyn spoke up. "But what about that hot-pink V-neck you got last year? That one really looks good on you."

I'd almost forgotten she was still in the room.

"Hot-pink V-neck?" I echoed. "Oh, right, I can't believe that one slipped my mind."

I dug into the drawer again. Aha, there it was. I'd bought the pink sweater at an end-of-season sale at the Alamo Quarry Market last spring, which meant I'd only had a chance to wear it once or twice. But Cait was right—I looked great in it.

I smiled at my sister in the mirror. "Thanks for the tip."

"Cool." She smiled back.

As I slipped on the sweater over a white T, I thought about Cait. Sure, she could be a pain sometimes with all the happy-shiny-bright-side stuff. But she was still my sister. Why should she get stuck in Nerd Central while I lived it up with the cool kids? Maybe once I was more firmly established in the popular crowd, I could start working her in, too.

Especially if she got over wanting to talk about our visions all the time.

Now that the visions had gotten me what I

wanted, I was ready for them to end. Or at least make sure they stayed out of my way.

WHEN I GOT to school, I stopped by my locker before heading to Megan's. The halls were crowded, and after dodging around a cluster of giggling seventh graders, I finally spotted her. She was leaning against the locker with Lavender, whispering and shooting looks at Gabe Campbell, who was swearing as he tried to wrestle open his locker nearby.

My eyes widened as soon as I got close. Lavender looked up and saw me, too, and her jaw dropped.

"Are you kidding me?" she exclaimed.

She was wearing my sweater! Okay, it wasn't *exactly* the same—hers was a crewneck with a little row of rhinestones around the collar. But it was pretty much the identical shade of hot pink.

Gabe finally managed to yank open his locker. He looked around defiantly, as if daring anyone to laugh or say anything. Then his gaze settled on me and Lavender.

"Whoa!" he blurted out with a laugh. "Check it

out—I guess Lavender caught some of the twins' crazy after all. Is that the new uniform for school losers?"

His loud, snorting laughter attracted attention from other kids, including Biff and Brent, who were horsing around nearby. The two jocks came closer.

"Hey, it's the Pink Ladies!" Brent said. "Can I join if I wear my pink sweater?"

"Aw, not fair," Biff joked. "Pink's totally not my color, dude!"

Lavender's poisonous glare settled on me. "You are *so* not wearing that today," she said icily. "Seriously."

"Whatever." I peeled off the V-neck quickly and shoved it into my bag. "It's way too hot for wool anyway."

So not true. My T-shirt was thin, and goose bumps were already rising on my arms. But I wasn't about to let that show.

Megan was glancing from me to Lavender with an uncertain smile. "Great minds think alike, right, girls?" she said.

Lavender already looked less annoyed now that my sweater was out of sight. "Yeah, well, some of us aren't interested in being a twin." She shot me an insincere smile. "No offense."

"It's okay." I glanced around, trying to gauge exactly how many people had witnessed our embarrassing moment. Luckily the B Boys had pretty short attention spans. But Gabe was still watching me, his face weirdly attentive. What was that about?

Then I saw that someone else was watching me, too. A little farther down the hall, I saw my sister lurking in a classroom doorway, looking my way with a slight grin on her face.

What was she doing there? Suddenly I had my suspicions. . . .

"CASSIE? HEY, EARTH to Cassie! What do you think—is it me?"

I realized I'd been spacing out, staring out the boutique window. Meanwhile Megan, Lavender, and Emily were trying on sunglasses and scarves and stuff.

Lavender watched me over a pair of rhinestone cat's-eye glasses. "Are you okay, Cassie? You act like you don't even want to be here."

Her tone was vaguely snotty. Ever since that morning's sweater incident, she'd been acting icier than ever toward me. Thanks, Caitlyn.

Because by now I was pretty sure my sister was behind the whole thing. She'd cajoled me into wearing that pink sweater—because she *knew* Lavender would be wearing one the same exact color today. How had she managed to touch Lavender long enough to have a vision? Cait seemed to be out to get me, and all because of the whole Liam thing.

I'd been on edge all day, waiting to see if she would pull anything else. Everyone knew Cait was a much slower burn than I was. But when she was pushed to her limit? Watch out.

I grabbed a pair of bright-green bug-eye glasses, forcing a grin. "How about these?" I put them on and struck a pose. "Are they me?"

Megan laughed. "Definitely. But only if you wear this, too." She jammed a hideous plaid hat on my head.

"No way." I pulled off the hat and tossed it aside, grabbing another one. "This is way better."

Lavender's eyes lit up. "Oh, look at that!" she exclaimed, her snippiness disappearing. "It's got little Scotties on it!"

I glanced at the hat. Sure enough, it was embroidered with a trio of tiny terriers. "Yeah, cute," I said. "Do you have a dog, Lavender?"

"Lav would have, like, a hundred dogs if she could," Emily said with a giggle. "But her parents only let her have one."

"His name's Amigo—I got him at the county shelter. He's the best." Then Lavender actually smiled at me. A miracle! But I knew I might have to rely on more than old-fashioned bonding.

"Cool," I said. "Want to try it on?" Deciding to take advantage of her better mood, I placed the Scottie hat on her head, brushing my thumb against her forehead as I adjusted it. Would that be enough to trigger a vision?

"Watch it," she said, her tone much sharper. "You practically poked me in the eye!"

"Sorry." I pulled my hand back quickly. This wasn't going to be easy.

Downtown Aura wasn't exactly a world-class shopping destination, but we made the best of it, fully exploring the three boutiques and handful of other stores. I even found out that Lavender's family owned the town's old-fashioned general store—which meant Lavender and her friends got free sodas from the cooler. Nice!

By the time I said good-bye to the others and headed for home, I'd almost managed to forget about Cait's revenge mission. But as I strolled through what passed for downtown Aura, my mind wandered back to what had happened. Now that I seemed to be stuck here, I had to make this town work for me. What if my sister messed up my plans? I had to deal with her somehow. . . .

But I pushed the thought out of my mind as I noticed someone hurrying along the sidewalk ahead of me. Someone familiar.

It was Gabe. He was walking fast, a small paper bag clutched in one hand. He hadn't seen me, which was good—the guy seemed to be a serious psycho.

Which made me think about that weird thing he'd said about Mom's job and the rest of it. What was that all about? Was there a way to find out? Come to think of it, Gabe looked a little suspicious rushing down the street clutching that bag....

I couldn't resist. Feeling a little too Nancy Drew for comfort but unable to fight my curiosity, I followed him.

I stayed about half a block behind Gabe as he walked around the corner and down the next street. When he turned again, I recognized the block we were on—it was the one where the police precinct was located. The rest of the block was mostly warehouses, small office buildings, and an empty lot, so there weren't many people around.

Weird, I thought. *If his uncle doesn't work there anymore, why's Gabe going to the cop shop?*

Or maybe he wasn't. As he neared the low-slung brick building, Gabe suddenly ducked into the narrow alley running beside it.

Uh-oh. Had he spotted me following him? I

hid behind a shrub across the street, feeling kind of stupid. But I definitely didn't want some kind of awkward confrontation with him right outside Mom's workplace.

I peered out of my hiding place just in time to see Gabe emerge again, only this time he wasn't alone. The man with him appeared to be around Mom's age; the seams of his blue shirt strained across his beefy shoulders, and he was wearing cowboy boots almost like Gabe's.

The two of them glanced around, and I shrank back so they wouldn't see me. A second later I looked out just in time to see Gabe hand over what looked like a small, lumpy gray brick. I had no idea what it was, but Gabe and Mr. Blue Shirt both seemed pretty happy about it. The man tucked the item into a canvas bag he was holding, then wiped his hand on his jeans and clapped Gabe on the back, both of them grinning and looking pretty pleased with themselves.

After that Gabe hurried off, disappearing around the corner. I didn't dare follow him with the other guy still standing there, so I stayed put. Finally the guy started to walk away, and I realized I needed to get moving, too. Mom was supposed to get out of work right around—well, now, actually. Just then she emerged from the precinct, laughing and calling something over her shoulder to whoever was just inside.

The man in the blue shirt heard her, too. He stopped short, then turned and took a few steps in her direction.

"You're sounding awfully cheerful, Officer Waters," he said loudly. "'Specially for someone who stole another man's job."

I froze. Uh-oh . . .

Mom looked confused for a second. Then her expression hardened into one of wary disdain.

"Charles Campbell, I presume?" she said icily.

"The one and only." Charles Campbell—Gabe's uncle Chuck!—hooked two fingers into his belt and swaggered another couple of steps forward. "You made a big mistake coming to this town, lady. We don't need outsiders here telling us what to do; you hear me?"

Mom looked annoyed now. "That's enough," she said. "I have things to do."

But Uncle Chuck stepped sideways, blocking her path as she tried to go around him. "Listen, Waters," he sneered. "I'm a nice guy, okay? All you gotta do is pack your things and hightail it back to the city, and I'll forget I ever heard of you and your family. Am I making myself clear?"

Was he threatening her—us? All Gabe's nasty comments flashed through my mind as I glanced at the precinct door, hoping another officer would come out. This guy seemed kind of unhinged. Mom needed help!

But the door stayed shut. Okay, if the cops weren't going to provide backup, I guessed it was up to me. At least I could scream pretty loudly if something happened. . . .

"Mom!" I blurted out, jumping into view from my hiding place. "I was in the neighborhood, so I figured I'd come walk you home."

Mom looked startled. "Cassie!" she said. "Hello."

"Hi." Not looking at Uncle Chuck, I slipped my hand into Mom's and squeezed, wanting her to know I had her back.

But as soon as I touched her, it happened again—my vision went fuzzy, and the buzzing filled my head, making me dizzy.

A second Mom appeared over the real one, but this Mom wasn't standing on the sidewalk next to me. She was inside the police station—with several uniformed officers in the background. The place looked dingy and kind of cramped, with a couple of small windows showing an angry, stormy-looking sky outside.

I stayed focused on Mom. She looked very upset as she grabbed things out of a desk drawer and tossed them into a cardboard box while an older man with a mustache glowered over her. Then I caught sight of his badge. It read, "Aura Police Chief."

I gasped and pulled away, and the vision was gone.

So was Uncle Chuck. In the time I'd been spaced out, he'd stalked away and was halfway down the block. I took a deep breath, hoping that Mom hadn't noticed me getting all quiet and weird on her.

"Are you okay?" I asked.

"I'm fine." She glared after Uncle Chuck, then glanced at me. "Come on, Cassie. Let's get home."

14
CAITLYN

WHEN I GOT home from school, nobody was there. I went into my bedroom and opened my computer. I'd been checking my email every chance I got, but there was still no response from that message board.

I decided to check the site again. I'd posted that message pretty quickly the other day. Maybe it hadn't gone through. Or maybe the email alert wasn't working right.

It was easy to find the parapsychology message board again. But when I started scanning the thread titles, the one I was looking for was nowhere on the first page. Strange. It had only been three days. But some message boards were pretty busy; maybe the thread had fallen out of sight, and that was why nobody was responding.

"Time to bump it," I murmured, clicking the arrow to go to the second page.

Once again I scanned the titles. Nothing. Checking the dates on some of the latest entries, I saw that they'd been posted last weekend.

With a frown, I clicked back to page one. The last date there was Monday afternoon. My thread should still be on the page. Had someone changed the title or something?

I read through the thread titles more carefully, trying to figure out if any of them might be the one I was looking for. This time I noticed a thread about three-quarters of the way down, titled simply "CLOSED."

I clicked to open it. My eyes widened when I recognized the name of the original poster from the "Real Psychics in the UK" thread. But the original post below the name was gone, replaced with a single, gray, italicized word: *deleted*. All of the posts that had followed the initial one, including mine, had disappeared.

I sat back and stared at the screen, my mind spinning. What did this mean? Why had the thread been closed and all the text deleted? It didn't make sense. Many of the other threads involved much crazier topics than this one. . . .

Just then I heard a clatter in the hall and clicked off the site. "Oh, good, you're home," Mom said as she poked her head into my bedroom. "Dinner in half an hour, okay?"

Cassie was right behind her. Her face was grim, and she didn't look at me as she entered the room. Gulp.

My satisfaction from that morning's sweater prank had worn off a little. I mean, Cassie totally deserved it after what she'd done to Liam. But I hated fighting with her—especially now, when all I wanted was for us to work together to figure out the vision thing once and for all.

It had been total chance that I'd seen Lavender wearing that hot-pink sweater at all. She'd turned up in the background of a vision I'd had in social studies the day before when Ms. Xavier rested her hand on my shoulder. It had been hard to miss that hot pink—or the big, loopy date written on the whiteboard. I'd barely even paid attention to what Ms. X herself was doing in the vision; she was smiling as the school secretary handed her a note.

"Come set the table in a few minutes, okay, girls?" Mom said, breaking me out of my thoughts. She glanced at the window. "Why don't you crack a window? It's stifling in here."

I climbed to my feet and headed for the window. "Are you sure we should open it?" Cassie said to Mom. "It's freezing out today. Definitely sweater weather."

She didn't so much as glance at me. But I winced at the extra emphasis she put on the word *sweater*.

"Up to you," Mom said. "Don't forget about setting the table."

As soon as she'd disappeared, Cassie turned to

face me. "Listen, Cait," she said. "We need to talk."

I braced myself—now there was no escape.

"You shouldn't have done that to Liam," I blurted out. "He never—"

"Forget it," she said sharply. "I'm sorry about it, really, and I'll try to make it up to him later, okay? But that's not important right now. I had another vision. And this one's about Mom."

"Huh?" That definitely wasn't what I'd been expecting her to say. "What did you see?"

"Something bad, I think." She started pacing, though our little bedroom only allowed about five steps before she had to turn around and go the other way. "It looked like she was at work, only she was really upset. I—I think she was packing up her desk. Like she'd been, you know, fired."

"What? Are you sure?"

"Pretty sure." She stopped pacing and sat down heavily on the edge of her bed, staring at me. "So what are we going to do?"

"Do?" I echoed. "Wait. Mom getting fired—isn't that what you *want* to happen? Without that job we'd have no reason to stay in Aura."

For a second my mind was filled with what that might mean. With nothing to keep us in Aura, Mom would probably move us back to San Antonio. We could return to our old school, our old friends, our old life. I'd been so busy trying to make the best of this move, support Mom, try to convince Cass that it wasn't the end of the world. All this time I hadn't allowed myself to think about anything else. But what if we could go home?

"I don't know," Cassie said, sounding uncertain. "I mean, I *thought* that was what I wanted. But Mom looked so unhappy in the vision—and I don't want *that*, you know?"

I pulled one leg up onto the edge of the bed, resting my chin on my knee. "She does seem to really love being a cop."

"She seems to like this crazy town, too, for some reason," Cass agreed.

I shot her a sidelong look. "And I kind of do, too," I said softly. "I mean, it's different from San Antonio—"

Cass snorted. "No kidding!"

"But it's not all bad, right?" I said. "The people are mostly nice. We both have friends now, and the teachers seem decent, you know? I mean, I think it's actually starting to feel like home."

"I might not go that far. But I guess this strange little place does have its good points." Cassie stood and starting pacing again. "I'm not saying I wouldn't rather be in San Antonio. But I don't want to move back if it means Mom has to give up her dreams."

I smiled at her. Maybe my sister and I still had a few things in common after all. "So what do we do?"

She stopped and looked at me. "Duh," she said. "We have to change the future. You said you think we can, right?"

"I said we *might* be able to," I corrected. "I mean, we just haven't tried it yet." I smiled at her, glad that we were talking again. Then my smile faded slightly. "So what do we do?"

"I don't know," she said. "But listen—I didn't tell you the rest of what happened. . . ."

By the time she finished her story about seeing Gabe and Uncle Chuck, my heart was thumping double time. "No way!" I blurted out, a little overwhelmed. "That sounds just like my vision!"

"Huh?"

"Remember when I tried to tell you about my latest vision earlier?" I said. "It was pretty much *exactly* what you just described."

I filled her in on the vision I'd had about Gabe and the unknown man—who apparently was his uncle Chuck. Cass listened, tilting her head to one side like she always did when she was super focused.

"Maybe the visions are connected," she said. "Why else would they meet up by the police station?"

Now that she'd said it, I suddenly felt uneasy, though I wasn't totally sure why. "I don't know," I said, sitting up straighter on the bed. "Why would it necessarily have anything to do with Mom, though? She wasn't even in my vision."

"Right. So why did Gabe and his uncle look so happy, unless they were out to cause trouble?"

"I don't know." I really, really didn't like the thought that Gabe and his uncle might be after

Mom for real. Couldn't there be another, less scary explanation for all this? "Wait! I just thought of something. What if what you saw wasn't really what you thought you saw?"

"What are you talking about?" Cassie said.

"Well, I never imagined that the vision I had about Megan would turn out to be something *good*, you know? For all we know, your vision about Mom could've been totally innocent. Like, maybe she was packing up her desk because they decided to give her a promotion and move her into her own office or something."

"Oh, I get it. Yeah." Cass looked thoughtful—and a little hopeful. "I mean, Mom looked pretty upset to me. But when I saw me and Brayden holding hands, I never thought *that* would end up the way it did either."

"So what if we're all worried for nothing?" I said. "Our two visions might have nothing to do with each other—or with anything bad."

"And what if we aren't?" she countered. "I mean, how often do the visions work that way?"

"I don't know." I leaned back on my bed, running through all my past visions in my head. "I never found out how most of them turned out. Like, that time I had the flu, but Mom was smiling. It could've been anything. Then there was the one at the dentist—all I know is that the hygienist was laughing, but I have no idea why." I ticked off each vision on my fingers. "The one with you and the test, well that wound up exactly as I saw it, since you aced it. And there was the one about Ms. Xavier yesterday, but it only showed her receiving a note in class, looking happy about it. And then it actually happened today, but I don't know what the note said."

Cassie leaned against the dresser, gazing at herself in the mirror. "Mine were mostly the same way: kind of cryptic and random. Like the food court guy at the mall looking scared, and the vision of Mom looking upset, and some girl at school crying—" Cutting herself off, she turned to face me, frowning. "Hey, I just realized something. All my visions show bad stuff: people that are sad, or worried, or poor Brayden breaking his leg."

"Really?" I thought about it. "Come to think of it, all mine so far have shown people looking happy or laughing. Even the one of Megan, which turned out to be positive, too, though it didn't look like it at first. What a crazy coincidence!"

"Or is it? What if that's the way it works? I see all the bad stuff, and you see only good stuff?"

"It's probably not like that," I said hurriedly. "I mean, how weird would that be?"

"Not weird. Just typical." She glared at me as if it was my fault. "I have to deal with the messy stuff, and you get to be Miss Sunshine all the time? How fair is that?"

"Quit it, Cass," I said. "Don't be so negative."

"Why not?" she snapped. "It sounds like that's what's supposed to happen."

This was veering offtrack fast. "Can we focus on this thing with Mom?" I said. As much as I was trying to stay optimistic, I couldn't shake the feeling that something was wrong—and that it might have to do with Gabe. "It's obvious now that Gabe isn't the only one who thinks Mom stole his uncle's job.

What if he and Uncle Chuck are trying to get Mom fired?"

Cassie was silent for a moment. "I guess it's possible," she said at last. "Anyway, it's our only clue so far. Maybe we should check him out—Gabe, I mean."

"Okay. But we won't see him until school on Monday."

"Or maybe tomorrow," Cass put in. "He'll probably be at the football game. We can try to question him there, maybe figure out what he and Uncle Chuck are up to."

I didn't like the thought of waiting. Not with something so important at stake. "The game's still a whole day away," I reminded her. "What if Mom gets fired today?"

Cassie looked alarmed, and I began to panic. Then she glanced at the window and shook her head. "She won't. What would they do? Call her back to work to fire her? And besides, the sky outside was super stormy in my vision," she said, looking suddenly relieved.

I followed her gaze. It was a bright evening, still

sunny without a cloud in the sky. "Are you sure?" I asked, still worried.

"Positive. We still have time."

"Good." I met her eyes and saw my own anxiety mirrored in her identical big browns. "Now all we need is to figure out what to do. And soon."

15

CASSIE

SATURDAY DAWNED GRAY and overcast. It wasn't as stormy as the sky I'd seen in my vision, but it looked to be heading in that direction. I couldn't help glancing at the window every few seconds as I picked at my cereal. It was pretty obvious that Cait had noticed it, too. She was a morning person, and normally drove me and Mom crazy being all chatty. But today she was as quiet as I was.

"What are your plans for today, girls?" Mom asked, sitting down with her second cup of coffee.

"Going to the big game?"

"Maybe." I shot another look at the window. "If it doesn't rain."

"It's supposed to hold off until tonight," Mom said. "Hope that's true, or it'll be a wet afternoon for all of us."

"What do you mean?" Cait asked. "I thought you had to work all day, Mom."

"I do." Mom sipped her coffee. "But I'm stationed at the games—the middle school first, then the high school game after."

"Really?" I traded a surprised look with Cait. "You mean you'll be *at* the football game?"

Mom nodded. "I'm told it's a tradition for all the officers to be at these games against the Jeffers teams. Just about the entire town will be there anyway, and emotions run pretty high—apparently this rivalry goes way back. Can't hurt to have a few extra cops there to keep an eye out for trouble." She winked at us over the rim of her mug. "Plus that way we don't have to argue over who gets time off to cheer on the home team." She checked her watch. "Speaking of work, I have to go."

She got up, leaving me staring at Cait across the table. It had been a long time since the days we claimed we could read each other's minds, but right now it wasn't hard to guess what she was thinking. What did this mean? If Mom wasn't even at the precinct, how could my vision come true?

I tried to tell myself this was good news, that it meant we had more time. But as I glanced at the steely sky outside, I couldn't quite make myself believe it.

"CASSIE! YOU'RE HERE!" Megan waved both arms over her head as I made my way toward her with Cait at my heels.

There was a pep rally held before the game, and it was still at least half an hour away. But it was obvious that the tailgate parties had started way early. Tons of people crowded the parking lot outside the stadium, sitting in lounge chairs, perched on truck tailgates, or just running around giddily. Music blared from every direction, along with the sounds of laughter and shouting. None of the partiers seemed to notice the still-threatening sky overhead. Pushing past some rowdy high schoolers, I finally reached my friends. They were gathered around Megan's sister's car. The hatchback was open, revealing lots of snacks and sodas laid out inside. Megan and the other cheerleaders were already in their uniforms, while everyone else was dressed head to toe in green and gold. I glanced around for Brayden, wondering if he might watch the game with us since he couldn't play. But there was no sign of him. Probably just as well—I didn't have time for distractions today.

"Hi, Cassie," Lavender greeted me, licking Doritos salt off her fingers. Then she noticed my sister behind me. "Oh, hi."

"Hi." Cait nudged me.

I cleared my throat. "Listen, we'll be right back, okay? I want to check out the scene." I forced what I hoped was a carefree laugh. "This is my first Jeffers game, and it's crazy!"

"I know, right?" Megan grinned and gave me a

high five. "Come back soon!"

"Promise." I tossed a smile to the whole group before diving back into the crowd.

Soon Cait and I were wandering the parking lot. "How are we going to find Gabe in all this?" she wondered breathlessly.

"You're the optimist—you tell me." I'd been thinking the same thing myself. This was way more intense than any football game I'd ever been to in San Antonio, and the crowd was only getting bigger!

We wandered around for a while with no luck. "What if Gabe doesn't come to the game?" Caitlyn said. "Liam and Bianca told me he got cut from the team—maybe he hates football now."

"Really? He's got to come. Otherwise we'll have to wait until Monday after all." I eyed the sky. "And somehow I'm thinking we don't have that much time."

"Oh, man, don't say that! Maybe we should— Wait! Is that him?" Cait grabbed my arm so tightly I winced.

But she was right. Gabe was sauntering through

the crowd just ahead, hands shoved in the pockets of his jeans.

"Gabe!" I called, sprinting forward. "Wait up!"

He turned, looking surprised to find me and Cait chasing him. "Oh, it's the twins," he said with a snort. "Fancy meeting you here."

"Yeah." I reached out and rested my hand on his arm. "Did you just get here?"

I was hoping for a vision that might help us, might tell us what to do next, but no luck. Gabe shrugged and stepped away, dislodging my hand. "What's it to you?"

"Oh, we're just excited. I mean, this is fun, isn't it?" Cait smiled and nudged him with her shoulder. I guessed she was trying to trigger a vision, too. Judging by the frustration that flashed in her eyes, I guessed it hadn't worked for her either.

Not that I was going to stop trying. "I like your watch," I said, grabbing his hand and pretending to admire the boring digital he was wearing. Rats! What good was having some freaky superpower if it didn't even work when you needed it? I took a deep breath, trying to calm my pounding heart.

Gabe glanced at my hand, then yanked his arm away, looking suspicious. "Why are y'all talking to me anyway?" he snarled. "Shouldn't you be hanging out with your dorky cheerleader friends?"

He stomped off, and I gritted my teeth. "Well, that was a bust. What are we supposed to do now?"

"I don't know." Cait looked anxious. "Let's try to keep an eye on him. It might be the only way to figure out if my vision and yours are actually connected."

I wasn't so sure. "We don't even know how all this hoodoo-voodoo stuff works," I reminded her. "It doesn't matter if we're with that loser for five seconds or five hours. Sometimes you get nothing."

"So you're just going to give up?" Cait said, a spark of challenge in her eyes. "But Mom—"

"Who said anything about giving up?" I interrupted. "But I do think it's time to give the spooky stuff a rest and do this the old-fashioned way. Wait here."

I strode off without giving her a chance to argue.

Gabe hadn't gone far—he'd stopped to watch a bunch of middle-aged men who were singing the Aura High fight song at the tops of their lungs. They'd painted their faces and chests green and gold, and one of them even had a pumped-up armadillo painted across his stomach.

But I ignored all that, zeroing in on Gabe. "Hey, why'd you run off like that?" I said, trying to sound friendly. "I was hoping we could talk more."

"Why?" he said, his tone halfway between belligerent and perplexed.

I giggled, hoping I sounded carefree rather than desperate and exasperated. We were seriously running out of time, and Mom's whole career could be at stake. "Because," I said, "you seem, you know, cooler than most of the guys at this school."

"Hmph." He still looked suspicious, but this time he didn't pull his arm away when I touched it.

Just then the PA system blared to life, calling everyone into the stadium for the pep rally. I waited until the cheers died away and people started pouring toward the entrance.

"Cool, it's starting," I said to Gabe. "Want to sit together?"

He only hesitated for a second, then shrugged. "Sure, I guess, whatever."

We passed Cait on the way in, and she fell into step behind us. Gabe barely seemed to notice her. He had his hands in his pockets again and was walking fast, nodding to people once in a while but not saying a word.

Soon we were inside. I spotted Mom standing with several other uniformed officers way down by the goalpost at the far end of the field. She was chatting and smiling, looking perfectly relaxed, and my stomach clenched as I flashed to the way she'd looked in my vision.

I glanced up. The clouds were scudding across the sky faster now, and it was getting dark.

"There's some seats," Gabe said, clambering up over the first few rows of bleachers without bothering to see if I was following.

I took my place beside Gabe, and Cait sat down on my other side. He shot her a suspicious look. "Is she sitting here, too?" he said.

"She doesn't have anyone else to sit with." I waited until Cait was looking the other way, then rolled my eyes, mouthing the word *nerd* at Gabe. Okay, I felt kind of bad about that, but it worked. Gabe snorted but looked amused.

Just then an older kid down on the sideline called his name, and Gabe turned away to shout back at him. Cait leaned closer. "Are you sure this is going to work?" she whispered.

"Ssh." I didn't want to make Gabe any more suspicious. If I could get him talking, maybe I'd be able to tell if he was up to anything. Or maybe I'd just mention Uncle Chuck and see how he reacted. I'd have to play it by ear.

The pep rally seemed to take forever. It was so loud that I couldn't get his attention, figuring things would quiet down a little once the game started. But with each second that ticked away on the big clock on the scoreboard, my anxiety ticked up another notch or ten. Every time I checked, the sky looked a little gloomier, the clouds a bit more threatening.

Was it as dark as it had been in my vision?

Finally the cheerleaders bounced off to the side-lines, and the home team ran in to a roar of approval from the crowd. As the players gathered on the side-lines, I saw Brayden hobbling out behind the rest on his crutches, his letterman jacket slung over his shoulders despite the warm, humid air.

Ugh. My heart sank. Seeing him made me feel even more freaked-out. That vision had come true and so would the one about Mom—unless Cait and I found a way to stop it.

As the game started, I tried talking to Gabe, but it was still so loud. How was I going to find out if he was involved in all this if we couldn't even hear each other? Finally I'd had enough. I told Cait to sit tight and leaned over to Gabe.

"Want to go get a soda? It may be quieter down there," I shouted into Gabe's ear.

He shot me a surprised look, as if wondering whether he'd heard me right. But then he nodded. Standing up, he shoved the girl in front of us in the shoulder.

"Coming through," he yelled, almost stepping on her hand as he went by.

"Sorry," I told the girl as I followed. "Excuse me."

A few minutes later Gabe and I were waiting in line for the concession stand. We could still hear the noise from the game, but it was muffled by yards of concrete.

"Whew!" I said, trying to hide my impatience. I had to get him talking—and fast. "That's better. Thanks for being such a, you know, gentleman."

"Yeah, sure." Gabe shrugged. "You're just lucky I'm not obsessed with football like most of the meatheads at this school."

I forced a smile. "You're definitely not like most guys, Gabe. You're much cooler."

"Glad you noticed." He took a step closer. "You're kind of cool, too."

He grabbed my hand and squeezed it. His palm was clammy and cold, and I immediately yanked my arm away.

"Ew!" I squealed, wiping my hand on my shirt.

His expression immediately turned into a scowl.

"Well, excu-u-u-use me, Princess Snotface!" he snapped.

"I never said you could touch me," I shot back before I could stop myself.

"Whatever," he snarled. "I was starting to feel sorry for you, but forget it. I'm glad you won't be around much longer. Just wait until Uncle Chuck gets through teaching your mama a lesson."

My whole body went cold. "What's that supposed to mean?"

He didn't respond, spinning on the heel of his cowboy boot and storming off without another word.

16

CAITLYN

"GOT YOUR TEXT," I said as I burst out of the stadium and found Cassie waiting for me by the concession stand. "Where's Gabe?"

"Gone." Cassie's face looked as stormy as the sky. "But you'll never guess what he said before he took off."

She filled me in, and my stomach sank. "Oh, no," I said. "It sounds like our visions really are connected somehow."

"Which means things are probably going down today," Cass agreed grimly, glancing up at the sky.

"We have to warn Mom!" I exclaimed.

Cassie hesitated. "Are you sure? What are we going to say, exactly?"

I'd already turned to hurry back inside, but now I stopped, realizing she had a point. "I don't know," I said. "But we have to tell her *something*. We can't just let this happen!"

"Whatever this is," Cass said. "We still don't know what's going on."

"But we know how it ends. Mom getting fired." I shook my head, tears coming to my eyes. "We have to stop it."

"I know. But how?" she said. "If we tell Mom we saw it happen in some freaky-deaky vision, she'll have us committed."

"So we don't tell her that part." I tugged on her sleeve. "Come on, there might not be much time."

"But . . . ," Cassie began.

Just then cheers erupted inside. The game was

still going on, but it was almost halftime.

"I have a plan," I lied. "Just follow along."

I started moving a little faster, and by the time Cassie caught up with me, Mom had eyed us from her spot near the scoreboard. She said something to her fellow cops and came forward to meet us.

"Hi, girls," she said cheerfully. "Having fun?"

"Sure," I blurted out. "But listen, we think you need to, um, go back to the precinct." I wasn't quite sure why I said it, but somehow it made sense. After all, it was where both visions had taken place.

"Huh? Why?" Mom looked startled.

I was out of ideas. When I shot Cassie a desperate look, she flashed me an annoyed one. But then she turned to Mom.

"We heard whispering in the stands. Something about some trouble," Cass said.

Mom furrowed her brow, studying each of us in turn. "What's this really about, you two?"

"Can't you just run over there?" I begged, feeling frantic as I saw the giant timer ticking down nearby. "It'll only take a minute. It's probably nothing, but . . ."

"But it could be something," Cass said firmly. "We're worried."

"You are?" Mom still looked confused. "Both of you? What did you hear, exactly? It doesn't sound like much to go on."

"I know," I said. "We just have a feeling about it, that's all."

"Yeah." Cassie glanced at me. "Call it twintuition."

Mom didn't respond for a second as her eyes bored straight into my head. Then she turned and did the same to Cass. I held my breath, certain she was going to tell us to stop wasting her time.

But finally she shook her head. "I could use a few minutes away from this din anyway," she said. "Wouldn't hurt to check on the place—just in case. Let me tell the others where I'm going."

None of us said much on the short ride through Aura's deserted streets. The place was like a ghost town. Every single person seemed to be at the game. As we turned the corner onto the street where the precinct was located, I saw Cassie clutching the armrest in the front seat.

A second later Mom finally spoke. "Who's that?" she muttered.

I leaned forward from the backseat, looking at the station ahead, its brick exterior dull beneath the cloudy sky. Not a single car was parked in the small lot, but a man in a blue shirt—just like the one in my vision—was opening the front door.

"Uncle Chuck!" Cassie blurted out.

Mom barely seemed to hear her. "That door is supposed to be locked!" she exclaimed. "Girls, stay right here."

She grabbed the dashboard radio and barked out an order for backup. Then she swung out of the car, her hand on her pistol.

"Stop right there!" she shouted, rushing toward the man.

Cassie and I traded a wide-eyed look. "Whoa," I said. "Go, Officer Mom! Go!"

Cassie opened the car door. "Come on," she said.

"We can't!" I said. "Mom said to stay here."

She ignored me, sprinting after Mom. I hesitated only for a second, then followed.

When we caught up, Mom was facing off against Uncle Chuck. "What are *you* doing here?" she demanded. "You don't work here anymore as far as I'm aware. And the precinct's closed."

"Doesn't look like it to me." Uncle Chuck jerked his chin toward the open door. "Looks to me like someone was careless. Weren't you the one who was supposed to lock up?"

"How did you know that?" For a second Mom looked confused. Then her face cleared. "Wait a minute. Just as we were leaving, I got called back in for a phone call. But when I picked up, nobody was there."

"It was him!" I blurted out. "Uncle Chuck. He probably called so you'd be the last one out!"

"Huh?" Uncle Chuck glanced at me. "What'd you call me, young lady? I ain't your uncle."

"We know your nephew," Cassie told him. "He

helped you with this whole plan, didn't he?"

Mom looked confused again. "Girls," she said sharply. "I thought I told you two to stay in the car."

"Yeah, you girls should listen to your mama." Uncle Chuck's glare was poisonous. "If you were mine, I'd teach you a lesson."

"That's enough," Mom snapped. "Now why don't you tell me what you're doing here, Mr. Campbell?"

"We can tell you, Mom," Cassie spoke up again. "He's trying to get you fired."

"Yeah," I said, my mind already working the angles. "I bet he was going to go in, maybe steal something or just mess stuff up. Then when everyone got back after the game later, you'd get blamed for forgetting to lock up on your way out."

Was I imagining things, or did Mom look impressed?

Actually, Cassie looked kind of impressed, too.

"Cait's right," she said. "That's exactly what he was planning. And his nephew Gabe was in on it, too."

"What?" Uncle Chuck shook his head quickly.

"That's crazy. Leave my nephew out of it. He's got nothing to do with any of this."

I bit my lip, thinking again of my vision of Gabe and Uncle Chuck outside the station. The vision that Cass had seen come true yesterday. I still had a strong feeling it was all connected to this, but how?

"So does that mean you're admitting the rest?" Mom asked Uncle Chuck sharply.

He glared at her, and then, slowly, he turned to us. "I ain't admitting nothing," he muttered. "Far as anyone knows, I was just wandering by and noticed the door was open."

I was standing a little to one side and saw that Uncle Chuck was fiddling with something behind his back. The glint of metal caught a weak ray of sunlight peeking through the clouds. Could that be . . . ?

I thought fast. "Hey, look out!" I yelped suddenly. "Is that a rattlesnake?"

All three of them jumped, startled. "Where?" Uncle Chuck said.

I heard a soft *clink* as something hit the ground.

Uncle Chuck dived for what he'd dropped, but I was faster.

"Hey, look what you dropped," I said, holding it up. "A key! What do you wanna bet it fits the lock right here on the station door?"

"How did you get that?" Mom asked. "Only current employees—"

"I'm not saying nothing!" Uncle Chuck yelled, his face going bright red. "I'm a lifelong officer of the law—I know my rights!"

Mom rolled her eyes. Then she stepped toward me to take the key, keeping one eye on Uncle Chuck. "How did you girls figure out what he was up to?" She glanced at him. "Allegedly, that is, of course." Her eyes flicked back to us. "Come to think of it, how'd you know I should head back here right now?"

Cass and I traded a look as I heard the sound of a siren coming fast. "Oh, it was nothing," I said. "Just a bit of twintuition."

THE NEXT FEW minutes passed in a whirl of confusion. Cassie and I stood back and watched as the police chief arrived, along with several other officers.

"He looks just like he did in my vision," Cass whispered as the chief strode over to confront Uncle Chuck.

Just then Mom noticed we were still there. "You two—back to the game," she ordered. "I'll take you."

The chief overheard her and looked our way. "No, you stay, Waters," he called. "One of the boys will drive them."

Despite our protests, we were herded into a car, and a tall, skinny young officer climbed into the driver's seat. "I feel like a prisoner," Cassie complained, leaning forward to peer at him. "You didn't even read me my rights!"

The young cop grinned. "You have the right to remain silent," he said. "But I got a couple girl cousins your age—and I know that ain't likely to happen."

I couldn't help laughing. "Can you blame us?" I said. "We just helped stop, like, a totally dramatic crime."

"Yeah." The young officer's smile faded, and he looked troubled. "Who'da thought Chuck would go all breaking-and-entering like that? Wonder what he was up to?"

"I guess we'll find out," I said, glancing at Cass.

When we arrived at the game, the fourth quarter had just started. Lavender was waiting for us right outside the bleachers.

"What happened?" she demanded. "Everyone's saying you guys just busted Chuck Campbell while he was trying to burn down the police station."

Cassie and I traded a look. "Not exactly," Cass said. "But Chuck's in big trouble anyway."

"No surprise there," Lavender muttered with a grimace.

"What do you mean?" I asked. "Do you know him?"

She shrugged. "Everyone in Aura knows him. The Campbells are always strutting around like they own this town."

She sounded annoyed. Remembering what I'd heard about Lavender's family, I guessed there might be some kind of competition between the Campbells and the Adamses. At least in Lavender's mind.

"Okay," Cassie was saying. "But I thought he was a cop."

Lavender pursed her lips and glanced around. "I shouldn't be telling you this. Can I trust you?" Her cool gaze rested on me.

"Cross our hearts," Cassie said. "Spill it!"

Lavender leaned closer. "Most everyone in town thinks Chuck left the force on his own," she said. "But Megan's uncle is the chief of police and her mom is the mayor, and—"

"Really?" I broke in. "Wow!"

"Yeah." Lavender shot me a look that told me exactly what she thought of being interrupted. "Anyway, Megan told me the real reason Chuck left is he got caught embezzling."

I gasped. "Embezzling?" I said. "You mean, like, stealing money from the town?"

"I guess. So since he came from such a good family and all"—Lavender paused just long enough to roll her eyes—"the chief kept it all hush-hush. Didn't want a scandal."

Lavender looked disappointed. I guessed she

was the type of person who loved a scandal. "Wow," Cass said. "That's heavy. I wonder—"

"Hey!" an angry voice interrupted.

Uh-oh. It was Gabe. He was barreling toward us, looking ready to explode.

"Yikes," Cassie said. "Um, maybe we should go inside? You know—where there are some witnesses around?"

Cassie, Lavender, and I ducked into the stadium. Gabe caught up with us there.

"What did you do?" he shouted, giving Cassie a shove on the shoulder that sent her staggering back.

"Calm down," I told him, glancing at the nearest set of bleachers. Several people were looking our way, attracted by the shouting. "We're not the ones who did anything. All we did was—"

"Shut up!" He whirled on me, his eyes so angry it was scary. "Just shut up, okay? Nobody wants you here anyway, so why don't you go back where you came from?"

"Speak for yourself, loser," Lavender said loudly. "I'd rather have Cassie here than your sorry behind."

Suddenly remembering me, she shot me a glance. "Uh, and her sister, too."

Gabe ignored her, glaring at Cassie again. "Was this why you were following me around earlier?" he demanded. "I shoulda known. You big-city girls are always trouble." He reached out as if to shove her again.

Cassie jumped back. A second later I heard the squeak of crutches over the sounds of the game. It was Brayden Diaz, hobbling toward us on his one good leg.

"Yo, Campbell!" Brayden's voice was deeper and sterner than usual. "What are you doing? Get away from her—uh, them."

"Who's gonna make me?" Gabe's chin jutted out, and he clenched his fists.

By now more people were watching us from the stands. "Fight! Fight!" a few guys chanted.

"Whack him with your crutch, Diaz!" a girl shouted with a laugh.

The ruckus caught the attention of the high school principal, who was sitting nearby. He hurried toward us. "Break it up!" he said sternly. "What's going on over here, young men?"

I stepped closer to Cassie. "Whoa," I murmured. "Knight in shining armor much? Is there something you need to tell me about you and Brayden?"

"Grow up," she said. "Can't a guy just be a gentleman without you getting all weird about it?"

Her voice sounded cool. But I knew her pretty well. Was that a hint of a blush creeping over her cheeks? Interesting . . .

The principal sent the boys back to their seats, watching to make sure nothing happened.

"Come on." Lavender poked Cassie on the arm. "You guys already made me miss, like, half the game. Let's go watch the rest."

"I STILL CAN'T believe nobody told Mom until now what really happened to the guy she replaced." That night Cassie leaned back on her pillow, hands tucked behind her head. "Didn't they think she might want to know that he got fired for embezzling?"

Yeah, Lavender's gossip turned out to be true.

Mom had confirmed it over dinner.

"I guess the chief was trying to protect him," I said. "At least that's what Mom said. The Campbells have been in Aura for, like, generations."

"That won't help Chuck now." Cassie sounded satisfied. "Mom said the chief is going public with what happened, and Chuck might end up in jail."

"Or at least pay a big fine or something," I added.

"I hope it's jail," Cassie said. "If he's free, he might try to cause more trouble for Mom."

"I doubt it." I rolled over and stared up at the shadows dancing on the ceiling. "The other officers know he was trying to make Mom look bad to get her fired. He won't be able to get away with anything, no matter what he does."

"Guess you're right. Besides, everyone would automatically suspect him if there's any more trouble."

Luckily, Uncle Chuck hadn't put up a fight when Mom arrested him for breaking into the locked precinct. It turned out that Uncle Chuck had had a copy of a key made. But nobody knew how he'd gotten his hands on a key to make the copy—nobody except me and Cassie. I'd remembered that visit from Gabe, the way his hand had felt sticky when I'd touched it. And she'd remembered that grayish brick of something or other she'd seen him pass to his uncle—and realized it looked a lot like the modeling clay from art class. He must have used it to make an impression of Mom's key when I had gone to get Mom from the backyard.

"Gabe was lucky Mom's keys were sitting right there when he stopped in," I mused aloud. "I mean, what was he planning to do otherwise?"

Cassie's snort echoed in the dark room. "I'm sure he would've come up with something," she said. "Asked for a glass of water to get her out of the room, maybe. He's sneaky, that one. Even Lavender says so."

I supposed she was right. "I just wish there was a way we could prove Gabe was involved."

"We can't," Cass responded immediately. "And we can't even try—not without making ourselves sound like mental cases."

Cassie was right—nobody would believe how

we knew about Gabe's involvement, even if we told them. It was still kind of hard to believe it myself.

"Speaking of our visions . . . ," I began.

Cass sighed. "Do we have to?" But there was no force behind her words this time.

"No, listen," I insisted. "This proves it can be done. We can change what we see! Isn't that kind of cool?"

I rolled over and peered through the darkness, but I couldn't see her face well enough to read it.

"It *is* cool," she said quietly after a moment. "But scary, too. You know?"

"Yeah. But that's even more reason to figure out what's happening to us." I thought about the parapsychology website and that deleted thread. Finding out more might not be easy, but that wasn't going to stop me. Especially with our twelfth birthday coming up so soon.

Cassie seemed to read my mind—just like old times. "I know you're going to do it no matter what I say, so I might as well go along with it." She sighed loudly.

I smiled in the darkness. I realized I hadn't told Cass about the website stuff, but that could wait until tomorrow. "True. It'll definitely be more fun arguing with you about it than going at it alone."

She laughed. "Face it—you love arguing with me!"

"I do," I admitted. "And Cass?"

"Yeah?"

"This has been fun. Working together, I mean. Like old times. Maybe moving to Aura hasn't been all bad, you know?"

"Yeah." There was a rustling across the room, and a moment later she jumped onto my bed, embracing me in a big hug. "It definitely hasn't been all bad."

I hugged her back, squeezing hard. As I did, my head filled with buzzing. The darkness cleared, and I saw a vivid vision of Cassie standing on the front porch. I was there with her. Both of us were looking at a package that Cass was holding. It was covered in foreign stamps and addressed to the two of us, but I couldn't quite make out the return address.

Cassie pulled back sharply, gasping. "Whoa," she

said. "I just had a vision—about *you!*"

"I had one about you, too," I said as the buzzing faded away. "What did you see?"

"The two of us were out front looking at a package."

I gasped. "With airmail stickers and stuff on it?"

Her face was only inches away, and her widened eyes caught the dim moonlight coming in through the windows. "You saw the same thing?" she exclaimed.

"Sounds like it." My eyes met hers, a mirror image of confusion. "But how's that even possible if I've been seeing positive stuff and you've been seeing negative stuff? It can't be good *and* bad at the same time, can it?"

"I don't know." She sounded a little nervous. "But when it does happen, good or bad, we'll have to deal with it."

"Right. We'll deal with it." I smiled and leaned in for another hug. "Together."

Turn the page for a sneak peek at what these
psychic sisters are up to in book two,
Double Trouble!

CAITLYN

"DID YOU GUYS ever hear of the Birthday Paradox?" Liam asked through a mouthful of half-chewed rice.

I added another dab of hot sauce to my burrito. It was Tex-Mex Thursday, and even though I'd only been at Aura Middle School for a little over three weeks, I'd already learned to ask the cafeteria ladies for extra spice. Nothing bums me out like a bland burrito.

"The birthday what?" I said.

"The Birthday Paradox." Bianca didn't bother

looking up from her book, which she was reading between bites of food. "Yeah, I've heard of it."

"Not me." I shrugged. "What is it?"

"It's an equation that proves if you have twenty-three random people in a room, there's a fifty-percent chance at least two of them will share the same birthday," Liam said. "It's a probability theory."

Typical Liam—he was supersmart, but unlike most supersmart people, he assumed everyone was just as smart as him. It was sweet, though occasionally confusing—sort of like Liam O'Day himself. I considered myself lucky that he'd been the first friend I'd made after moving to Aura, Texas. He'd introduced me to Bianca Ramos, who was just as nice, though a lot quieter.

"Twenty-three people, huh?" I capped the hot sauce. "In my house, all we need is two people to make it a hundred-percent chance—as long as those two people are me and Cassie."

Liam let out his snorty laugh, flipping his messy red hair off his forehead. "Good one, Caitlyn!"

Bianca glanced at me. "It must be weird sharing

your birthday with a twin."

"Not really." I shrugged. "I mean, not to us. We're used to it, you know?"

"So what are you going to do to celebrate the big 1-2?" Liam asked.

"Not sure yet. My birthday kind of snuck up on me this year." I poked a black bean back into my burrito. "Cass and I usually throw a party together or something, but we haven't even talked about it yet."

My gaze wandered across the crowded cafeteria. My sister was sitting at the big table dead smack in the middle of the room, where the most popular sixth graders hung out.

That was new. At least sort of. For the first week or so after we'd moved to this tiny town, Cassie had seemed determined to live up to the *lone* in "Lone Star State." No friends, no fun, no way. She was that sure we'd be moving back to San Antonio once our mother realized how lame this place was. It had never seemed to occur to her that Mom might actually *like* living in a small town. Or that I might. Or that she might not totally hate it herself.

Then again, I wasn't too shocked by her reaction. The move had been a surprise for both of us, and Cassie didn't always handle surprises that well. Oh, don't get me wrong—we were both used to moving. Mom had been in the army since before we were born, which meant we'd lived all over the country.

But we'd been in San Antonio for almost three years—a record for us. When Mom retired from the military and went to the police academy, we'd figured the city was home sweet home for good. Things didn't turn out that way, though. There weren't any open spots on the force there, and Mom had landed a job in Aura instead.

I'd tried to make the best of things from the start. It's just what I do. Cassie? Not so much. Our mom says she was born looking for the dark cloud behind the silver lining. She could be stubborn as a three-legged mule, too. And she'd been certain from the start that living in Aura was going to be about as pleasant as wet socks. To be honest, I still wasn't sure what had changed her mind. But I was glad she'd finally decided to fit in. And not at all surprised that she'd wormed her way into the popular crowd lickety-split.

Liam's gaze followed mine over to Cassie. "Do you share your presents, too?" he asked.

"No way," I said. "Good thing. Cassie and I don't exactly have the same taste, if you hadn't noticed."

Not anymore, anyway. Once upon a time, we'd loved being twins. We'd been best friends and done everything together. We'd even dressed alike as often as Mom would let us.

When had that changed? I couldn't quite recall. These days we still looked alike, with matching big brown eyes and skinny legs. But everything else about us was different.

Okay, wait. Maybe we did have one other thing in common lately. One *major* thing.

"So what about your dad?" Liam asked. "Does he visit or send you stuff on your birthday?"

I blinked, startled. "My dad?"

Bianca nudged Liam. "Don't be so nosy," she muttered. "We don't even know if . . ." She glanced at me and shrugged. "You never talk about your father."

True enough. "Yeah, sorry. I probably should've

said something sooner." I tried to sound normal. "He died years ago. When Cass and I were babies."

"Oh!" Liam's eyes widened. "I just figured your folks were divorced like mine. Sorry."

"Yeah, me, too," Bianca said softly, not quite meeting my eyes.

For a second she looked really sad and sort of distant, which was kind of weird. As far as I knew, both her parents were still totally alive and happily married right there in Aura, Texas. Maybe she was thinking about a grandparent who'd passed on or something. Whatever—I wasn't going to pry. Especially since I didn't want them to ask me any more questions either. Like how my dad died, or what he'd done for a living, or what he was like. Little stuff like that. None of which I knew the answer to. Weird, right?

But that was how it was. For as long as I could remember, our mom had refused to talk about him. No matter what we asked, all she'd say was, "We'll discuss it when you're older." For some reason, she'd made up her mind that the whole topic was off-limits. And when Deidre Waters set her mind to something, it stayed set. Period, full stop, and woe to the girl who tried to push her.

Just about all Cassie and I knew about our dad was that his name was John Thompson, and that Mom met him while she was stationed overseas when she first joined the army. We also knew that he was white, with sandy hair and a square jaw. But only because Cassie talked me into sneaking into Mom's room when we were six or seven and peeking at the wedding photo packed away in a big box on the top shelf that we were *absolutely not* supposed to touch. Mom never found out about that. At least we don't think she did. Although the next time Cass tried to find that box, it was gone, so who knows.

Anyway, since Mom wouldn't tell us anything, Cass and I made up all kinds of wild, crazy, romantic stuff about our dad. Like that he was an international spy who saved the world on a regular basis. Or a pirate who robbed from the rich and gave to the poor. Or a movie star who was always off shooting fabulous films in exotic locations. But lately, we didn't talk to each other about our father much. What was the point?

"I'll have to get with Cass about next weekend's party plans," I told my friends, taking a bite of my burrito as I changed the subject. "Whatever we're doing, y'all are invited for sure."

I hoped Cassie was okay with that. She seemed to think my new friends were nerds. So what if they were? I liked them, and that was all that mattered.

Liam stabbed a stray bean with his fork. "Maybe you guys should do a movie party. You could make it a monster movie theme and tell people to come in costume. I still have this awesome Godzilla suit from last Halloween."

I grinned, imagining what Cassie would say to that idea. As tough as she liked to act, scary movies freaked her out. Even cheesy monster ones.

"I'll take it under advisement," I told Liam, scooping up all the hot sauce that had dripped out of my burrito. "Any other ideas?"

"There's a new minigolf place over on the other side of Six Oaks."

"Hmm." Miniature golf actually sounded kind of fun. I made a mental note to mention it to Cass. "Okay, that's another one for the list. Next?"

As usual, Liam was full of ideas, and we spent the rest of lunch discussing party plans. Bianca had less to say, though she did veto Liam's suggestion of an insect cuisine cook-off—apparently he'd seen something on TV about how nutritious and ecologically correct it was to turn our six-legged friends into a major part of our diet.

I had to agree with Bianca on the bug thing. Otherwise I didn't care what we did as long as everyone had fun. I couldn't wait to figure out a plan with Cassie—just like old times.

The thought made me smile. That was one good thing about the crazy stuff that had been happening to me and Cassie lately. It had brought us together again, just when I was afraid she'd drifted so far away I barely knew her anymore.

As I followed my friends out of the cafeteria, someone grabbed my arm. It was Ms. Xavier. She was my homeroom teacher and also taught social

studies. With her wild, wavy hair, jangling bracelets, and flowing boho skirts, she stood out among
the other teachers like a peacock among chickens.
Her style wasn't really my thing, but I had to admire
her for following her own drummer.

"Cassie Waters!" she exclaimed in her loud,
enthusiastic voice. "I wanted to talk to you before—
oh!" Her kohl-lined eyes widened, and she laughed.
"Sorry, Caitlyn. I thought you were your twin for a
second."

I smiled politely. Cass and I used to get mistaken
for each other all the time back in the days when we
dressed alike and wore our hair the same way. Now?
Not so much. Most people caught on quickly that
Cass was the sister who was always decked out in
the latest fashions, while I was the one who went for
a more comfortable, classic look. But like I said, Ms.
Xavier's personal style was so far out there that she
probably didn't really notice the difference.

"I think Cassie already left." I hoped Ms. Xavier
wasn't looking for Cass because of some kind of
problem. Social studies had never been one of my

sister's best subjects.

"It's all right; she has my class next," the teacher said. "I'll catch up with her there. But as long as I have you, Caitlyn, I want to talk to you, too."

"Um, okay." I hoped she didn't have too much to say. I had to head to math, and Ms. Church was tough on tardiness. "What is it?"

"Have you decided on a topic for your research project yet?" she asked.

Every sixth grader was supposed to do a written and oral report on a topic related to US history, society, or culture. Bianca already had her project on the Civil War half done, though most people were still in the planning stages since the project wasn't due for over a month.

"Um, not yet, but I'm narrowing it down," I said. "I was thinking about doing something on Lewis and Clark, or maybe the Alamo, since I used to live near—"

"Great, great," she broke in, nodding like a bob-blehead. "But before you settle on anything, I had a thought. Twins are such an interesting aspect of human society. Maybe you could do your project on well-known American twins? For instance, there are those twin astronauts, or the former mayor of San Antonio and his twin who became a congressman, and I'm sure there are others." She squeezed my elbow. "Perhaps you could even look into whether being a twin helped lead to their success."

"What do you mean?" I asked, a little confused. "How would being a twin make a difference?"

Her smile broadened. "Well, I was thinking about everything I've read and heard about twins having special powers and thought it be would be fascinating to look into that aspect of things, you know?"

I gulped, suddenly very aware of her hand on my arm. Special powers? She didn't know the half of it!

It had all started about six months earlier. I began getting visions of people when I touched them—whether it was a hug, a handshake, or just a brief pat on the arm—and these visions came true. It didn't happen every time I touched someone, but when it did, the person I was touching would fade away and be replaced by a different vision of that person. For instance, one time I'd been talking to Cassie when I suddenly got a vision of her coming home with an A on a test. And then a couple of days later, it had actually happened.

The first few times, I'd thought it was a coincidence—just a weird daydream or something. It was only after we moved to Aura that I discovered Cassie was having these visions, too, and we realized we were seeing the future.

If that didn't qualify as a special power, what did?

WILL CASSIE AND CAITLYN'S BIRTHDAY BE A TON OF FUN—OR A BIG FIASCO?

Find out in the twin-tastic sequel to
Twintuition: Double Vision by Tia and Tamera Mowry!